A *People* Book of the Week

"FRESH." —*Entertainment Weekly*

"WITTY." —*The New York Times Book Review*

"SWIFT." —*Chicago Sun-Times*

"SHARP." —*People*

"SNAPPY." —*Chicago Tribune*

"A WINNER." —*Kirkus Reviews*

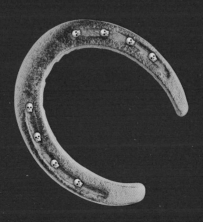

continued on next page . . .

PAPER DOLL

Spenser searches for the killer of a "model wife and mother"—and finds some shocking surprises. . . .

"IT TAKES ROBERT B. PARKER EXACTLY TWO SENTENCES TO GET THE TENSION CRACKLING."
—Christopher Lehmann-Haupt, *The New York Times*

DOUBLE DEUCE

Spenser and Hawk wage war on a street gang. . . .

"MR. SPENSER IS AT HIS BEST . . . TENSE . . . SUSPENSEFUL . . . DARKLY POETIC." —*The New York Times*

PASTIME

A boy's search for his mother forces Spenser to face his own past. . . .

"EMOTIONALLY TENSE . . . GRIPPING . . . VINTAGE HARD-CORE SPENSER!" —*Kirkus Reviews*

STARDUST

Spenser tries to protect a TV star from a would-be assassin. . . .

"CLASSIC SPENSER . . . BRILLIANT!"
—*The New York Times Book Review*

PLAYMATES

Spenser scores against corruption in the world of college basketball. . . .

"A WHOLE LOTTA FUN . . . KICK BACK AND ENJOY!"
—*New York Daily News*

PERCHANCE TO DREAM

Robert B. Parker's acclaimed sequel to the Raymond Chandler classic *The Big Sleep*, featuring detective Philip Marlow . . .

"A STUNNING, DROP-DEAD SUCCESS . . . DAZZLING."
—*Publishers Weekly*

HUGGER MUGGER

ROBERT B. PARKER

BERKLEY BOOKS, NEW YORK

HUGGER MUGGER

A Berkley Book / published by arrangement with
the author

PRINTING HISTORY
G. P. Putnam's Sons hardcover edition / April 2000
Berkley mass-market edition / June 2001

The Penguin Putnam Inc. World Wide Web site address is
http://www.penguinputnam.com

ISBN: 0-425-17955-9

BERKLEY®
Berkley Books are published by The Berkley Publishing Group,
a division of Penguin Putnam Inc.,
375 Hudson Street, New York, New York 10014.
BERKLEY and the "B" design
are trademarks belonging to Penguin Putnam Inc.

PRINTED IN THE UNITED STATES OF AMERICA

10 9 8 7 6 5 4 3 2 1

Joan: the ocean's roar, a thousand drums

HUGGER MUGGER

ONE

- -

I WAS AT my desk, in my office, with my feet up on the windowsill, and a yellow pad in my lap, thinking about baseball. It's what I always think about when I'm not thinking about sex. Susan says that supreme happiness for me would probably involve having sex while watching a ball game. Since she knows this, I've never understood why, when we're at Fenway Park, she remains so prudish.

My focus this morning was on one of those "100 greatest" lists that the current millennium had spawned. In the absence of a 100 greatest sexual encounters list (where I was sure I would figure prominently), I was vetting the 100 greatest baseball players list and comparing it to my own. Mine was of more narrow compass, being limited to players I'd seen. But even so, the official list needed help. I was penciling in Roy Campanella ahead of Johnny Bench, when my door opened and a man and woman came in. The woman was great to look at, blond, tight figure, nice clothes. The man was wearing aviator sunglasses. He looked like he might have a view on Roy Campanella, but I was pretty sure she wouldn't. On the other hand, she might have a view on sexual encounters. I could go either way.

"Good morning," I said, to let them know there were no hard feelings about them interrupting me.

"Spenser?" the man said.

"That's me," I said.

"I'm Walter Clive," he said. "This is my daughter Penny."

"Sit down," I said. "I have coffee made."

"That would be nice."

I went to the Mr. Coffee on the filing cabinet and poured us some coffee, took milk and sugar instructions, and passed the coffee around.

When we were settled in with our coffee, Clive said, "Do you follow horse racing, sir?"

"No."

"Have you ever heard of a horse named Hugger Mugger?"

"No."

"He's still a baby," Clive said, "but there are people who will tell you that he's going to be the next Secretariat."

"I've heard of Secretariat," I said.

"Good."

"I was at Claiborne Farms once and actually met Secretariat," I said. "He gave a large lap."

He smiled a pained smile. Horse people, I have noticed, are not inclined to think of horses in terms of how, or even if, they kiss.

"That's fine," he said.

Penny sat straight in her chair, her hands folded in her lap, her knees together, her ankles together, her feet firmly on the floor. She was wearing white gloves and a set of pearls, and a dark blue dress that didn't cover her knees. I was glad that it didn't.

"I own Three Fillies Stables. Named after my three daughters. We're in Lamarr, Georgia."

"Racehorses," I said.

"Yes, sir. I don't breed them, I buy and syndicate."

Penny was wearing shoes that matched her dress. They were conservative heels, but not unfashionable. Her ankles were great.

"In the past month," Clive said, "there has been a series of attacks on our horses."

"Attacks?"

"Someone is shooting them."

"Dead?"

"Some die, some survive."

"Do we have a theory?" I said.

"No, sir. The attacks seem entirely random and without motivation."

"Insurance scam?"

"Nothing so crude as shooting the horse," Clive said.

He was tall and athletic and ridiculously handsome. He had a lot of white teeth and a dark tan. His silver hair was thick and smooth. He was wearing a navy blazer with a Three Fillies crest on it, an open white shirt, beige linen trousers, and burgundy loafers with no socks. I approved. I was a no-socks man myself.

"Eliminate the competition?"

Clive smiled indulgently.

"Some of the horses who've been shot are barn ponies, not even Thoroughbreds—to think you could do anything constructive for your own horse, by eliminating other horses . . . not possible."

"Only a dumb city guy would even think of such a thing," I said.

He smiled again. It was a smile that said, *Of course I'm superior to you, and both of us know it, but I'm a good guy and am not going to hold it against you.*

"You're a detective, you have to ask these questions," he said kindly.

He smiled again. Penny smiled. I smiled back. Weren't we all just dandy. Penny had big eyes, the color of morning glories. Her eyes were nearly as big as Susan's, with thick lashes. Her smile was not superior. It was friendly . . . and maybe a little more.

"Last week, someone made an attempt on Hugger Mugger," Clive went on.

"Unsuccessful?"

"Yes. His groom, Billy Rice, was in the stall with him, at night. Hugger had been sort of peckish that day and Billy was worried about him. While he was there someone opened the stall door. Billy shined his flashlight and saw a rifle barrel poking through the open door. When the light came on, the rifle barrel disappeared and there were running footsteps. By the time Billy peeked out around the door, there was nothing."

"Footprints?" I said.

"No."

"Could he describe the gun barrel?"

"The gun barrel? What's to describe?"

"Did it have a magazine under the barrel, like a Winchester? Long stock or not? Front sight? Gun barrels are not all the same."

"Oh God," Clive said, "I don't know."

I tried not to smile a smile that said, *Of course I'm superior to you, and both of us know it, but I'm a good guy and am not going to hold it against you.*

"Cops?" I said.

"Local police," Clive said. "And I have my own security consultant."

"Local police are the Columbia County Sheriff's Department," Penny said. "The deputy's name is Becker."

"I wish to hire you, sir, to put a stop to this," Clive said.

"To prevent the horse from being hurt?"

"That certainly."

"Usually I get only one end of the horse," I said.

Penny laughed.

Clive said, "Excuse me?"

"Daddy," Penny said, "he's saying sometimes he gets a client who's a horse's ass."

"Oh, of course. Guess I'm too worried to have a sense of humor."

"Sure," I said.

"Well, sir, are you interested or not?"

"Tell me a little more of how you see this working," I said. "Am I sleeping on a blanket in the horse's stall, with a knife in my teeth?"

He smiled to show that he really did have a sense of humor even though he was worried.

"No, no," he said. "I have some armed security in place. An agency in Atlanta. I would like you to look at the security and let me know what you think. But, primarily, I want you to find out who is doing this and, ah, arrest them, or shoot them, or whatever is the right thing."

"And what makes you think I'm the man for the job?" I said.

Penny smiled at me again. She thought my modesty was very becoming.

"The horse world is a small one, sir. You were involved in some sort of case over there in Alton a few years back, with Jumper Jack Nelson. I knew of it. I talked with the Alton Police, with someone in the South Carolina State Attorney's Office. My attorney looked into it. We talked with the FBI in Atlanta. We talked with a man named Hugh Dixon with whom I once did some business. We talked to a Massachusetts State Police captain named Healy, and a Boston police captain named Quirk."

"How the hell did you find Hugh Dixon?" I said.

"I have money, sir. My attorneys are resourceful."

"And I'm the man?"

"Yes, sir, you are."

"Fairly expensive," I said.

"What are your fees?" Clive said.

I told him.

"That will not be an issue," he said.

"And who is the outfit in Atlanta that's on the job now?" I said.

"Security South."

Meant nothing to me.

"The on-site supervisor is a man named Delroy. Jon Delroy."

That meant nothing to me either.

"Will Mr. Delroy be pleased to see me?"

"He'll cooperate," Clive said.

"No," Penny said. "I don't think he will be pleased to see you."

Clive looked at her.

"Well, it's the truth, Daddy. He will be absolutely goddamned livid."

Clive smiled. He couldn't help being condescending, but it was a genuine smile. He liked his daughter.

"Penny has been quiet during our interview, Mr. Spenser. But don't assume that it's habitual."

"Jon will have trouble with you bringing in someone over him," Penny said. "Mr. Spenser may as well know that now."

Clive nodded.

"He's not really 'over' Jon," Clive said. "But Jon may feel a bit compromised. That a problem to you, Mr. Spenser?"

"No."

"Really?" Penny said. "You think you can work with someone like that?"

"I'll win him over," I said.

"How?"

"Northern charm," I said.

"Isn't that an oxymoron?" she said.

"You're right," I said. "Maybe I'll just threaten him."

TWO

"LAMARR, GEORGIA?" SUSAN said.

She was lying on top of me in her bed with her clothes off, her arms folded on my chest, and her face about six inches from my face. Pearl the Wonder Dog was lying somewhat grumpily on the rug at the foot of the bed, having been displaced, if only temporarily, by me.

"Just an old sweet song," I said.

"Don't sing. Do you know anything about race-horses?"

"Secretariat gave me a big lap once," I said.

"Anything less specialized?" Susan said.

"That's about it."

"And you are being brought in over someone who has heretofore been in charge?"

"Yes."

"So you are going to Georgia without Pearl, or me, and you'll be gone for who knows how long, and you don't know what you're doing, and the people you're working with will resent you."

"Exactly," I said.

"And you're doing this because you love horses?"

"Because I hate starving," I said. "I've been doing *pro bono* for you and Hawk so long that I can't afford to buy a new knuckle knife."

"Too bad virtue is not, in fact, its own reward," Susan said.

"Or if it really were, the reward would need to be monetary."

"Well, perhaps we can visit."

"You and Pearl could come down," I said.

"Pearl does not, obviously, fly in a crate in the hold of some disgusting airplane," Susan said.

"It's an easy drive," I said. "One overnight stop."

Susan stared at me. Her eyes were so close they were out of focus as I looked up at her. They seemed bigger than human eyes could be and bottomless, like eternity.

"I cannot bear to drive long distances."

"Of course you can't," I said. "Maybe Paul would come up from New York, for a weekend, and take care of Pearl."

"That might work," Susan said. "Or Lee Farrell, or Hawk."

"And then you can come to Lamarr on an airplane and ball my brains out."

"Didn't I just do that?" Susan said. "Except for the airplane part?"

"Yes," I said, "and brilliantly."

"I know."

"However," I said, "I don't think we've ever done it in Georgia."

"Well, if you insist on going down there," Susan said, "what's a girl to do?"

"What she does best," I said.

"In which case we'll never be able to eat lunch in Lamarr again," Susan said.

THREE

I SHOWED UP in Lamarr with some clean shirts and extra ammunition in my black Nike gym bag, checked into the Holiday Inn on the highway outside of Lamarr, and set out to visit my employer.

Lamarr was one of those towns you read about but no one you know ever lived in. It was probably like the town that Jack Armstrong lived in with his sister Betty, when he starred at Hudson High. The downtown was three-story buildings, mostly brick, along the main street, with some stores and restaurants, a pool hall, a movie theater, and a railroad station. There were two cross streets, where more business was done during daylight hours. In the center of the town was a square with a statue of a man on horseback, and some benches. As I drove through the downtown, the streets were lined with trees, and behind the trees were lawns on which sat some nice-looking southern-type houses, mostly white, with verandas. Often vines grew over the verandas and made them leafy.

At two in the afternoon I was ringing the bell at the Clives' front door. They lived in a white mansion with a wide pillared veranda across the front, which sat in the middle of something that looked like the world's largest putting green. A sprinkler system was producing a fine spray to protect the lawn from the East Georgia summer, and the sun shining through the spray made it iridescent.

Penny Clive, in white shorts and a blue top that didn't quite conceal her belly button, answered the door. All of her that I could see uncovered was a smooth tan. Not the deep-cured kind, but a gentle healthy-looking one that seemed casually acquired, though the evenness of it made me wonder just how casual the process was.

"Well, hello," she said.

She had a light voice with some kind of rich undertone, which made everything she said imply somewhat more than it seemed to. I had a moment when I thought maybe it wasn't so bad that Susan couldn't be here. I thought about whether I should feel guilty about that and decided I should not since I was simply being human, albeit male human.

"Hello."

"Please come in. Do you have everything you need at the hotel?"

We stood in a vast, high central hallway with dark floors that gleamed with polish.

"Bed, television, a/c, running water, what more could there be?" I said.

"What indeed?" she said, and the little smile lines at

the corners of her wide mouth deepened. "I was just having some iced tea on the terrace—would you have some with me?"

"Of course," I said, and followed her the length of the corridor and out through some very large French doors onto a wide white-brick terrace under a green-and-white-striped canvas canopy.

"Daddy's not here," she said.

"You're more fun anyway," I said.

"It depends," she said.

She gestured at a couple of comfortable-looking patio chairs. We sat. There was a big glass pitcher on a serving table and some glasses and ice in a bucket and sugar and lemons and fresh mint.

"On what?" I said.

"On whether you're a business partner or a sex partner," she said.

She put ice in a tall glass, added a lemon wedge and a mint leaf, and poured me some iced tea. I added some sugar.

"It's probably not the business partners who are voting for fun," I said.

"No," Penny said. "Speaking of fun, we're having a little welcome party for you tonight. I hope you don't mind."

"Most employers hold one when I leave," I said.

"Daddy thought it would be a convenient way to introduce you to everybody. Very informal, starts around seven."

"Wouldn't miss it," I said.

The backyard, if one could call it that, was being

sprinkled too. It stretched dead level toward some sort of outbuildings in the middle distance. Beyond them was a tennis court and, beyond the courts, a paddock and what I assumed were stables. As we sat, a Dalmatian came sniffing around the corner of the terrace, paused, looked up, put his ears back, and came over toward me, moving more slowly, with his head lowered a little and his tail wagging tentatively.

"That's Dutch," Penny said.

Dutch kept coming until he was in pat range. I put my closed fist out so he could sniff it. Which he did for maybe a full minute, quite carefully sniffing all aspects of it. Then he was satisfied. His ears came back up and his tail resumed full wag. He put his head on my leg and stood while I stroked his head.

"Tell me more about the horse shootings," I said.

She was turned half sideways in her chair, one leg tucked under her, giving me her full attention. She was clearly one of those especially likable women who made you feel that you might be the most interesting creature they had ever encountered. I knew that everyone she talked to felt that way, but it was no less pleasing for that. Right now it was my turn.

"I'm not sure where to start," she said. "I know all of us are in something of a tizzy."

"Well, were all the horses shot with the same weapon?"

"Oh God, I wouldn't know that sort of thing. Jon Delroy might know. Or you could talk with Deputy Becker."

"Any geographical pattern?"

"All here," she said.

"How many horses?"

"Three—a stable pony, and two colts."

She sipped some iced tea, dipping her face into it, holding the glass in both hands, looking at me over the rim.

"Where did they get shot?"

"I just told— Oh, you mean what part of them did the bullet hit?"

"Yes."

"One in the head, the stable pony. He died. Heroic Hope was shot once in the left shoulder. I don't think he'll run again. Saddle Shoes was shot in the neck. The vets tell us he should be fine."

"You said 'bullet'—was each of them shot just once?"

"I believe so."

Dutch took his head off my leg suddenly and walked away. I saw no reason for it. He appeared to be stepping to the beat of his own drummer. He found a spot on the lawn, in the sun, out of sprinkler range, turned around three times, and settled down and went to sleep.

"Only one died?" I said.

"Yes."

I nodded.

"You're looking so wise all of a sudden. Have I supplied you a clue?"

"Just a thought," I said.

"Oh, tell me, what is it?"

I shook my head.

"I assume that's not Three Fillies world headquarters down there," I said.

"The stables? Oh God no. It's where we keep our own horses. The racing operation is about a mile down the road. Are we changing the subject?"

"Yes, ma'am."

"So you won't have to tell me your thought?"

"I have so few," I said. "I like to nurture them."

She nodded thoughtfully and sipped a little more of her tea.

"You're very charming," she said. "But you don't actually say very much."

"I haven't much to say."

"I don't believe that," Penny said.

"And detectives get further listening than they do talking."

"Are you being a detective now?"

"I'm always being a detective," I said.

"Really? Is that how you define yourself?"

"No. I define myself as Susan Silverman's main squeeze. Detective is what I do."

"Are you married to her?"

"Not quite."

"Tell me about her."

"Smart, a little self-centered, intense, quick, very tough, very funny, dreadful cook, and beautiful."

"What does she do?"

"Shrink."

"Wow."

"Wow?"

"Well, I mean, it's so high-powered."

"Me too," I said.

Penny smiled.

"Have you two been together for a long time?" she said.

"Yes."

"But you've never married."

"No."

"Is there a reason?"

"It's never seemed a good idea at the times we've thought about it."

"Well, I'd love to meet her."

"Yes," I said. "You would."

When the sprinklers stopped, Penny and I took a stroll with Dutch around the grounds, the tennis courts, and the riding stables. The unexplained outbuildings turned out to be a small gymnasium with weight-lifting equipment and two locker rooms. Then I went back to my hotel to think long thoughts. As is usual when I'm thinking long thoughts, I lay on the bed with my eyes closed. Susan says I often snore when thinking long thoughts.

FOUR

- - - - - - - - - - - - - - - - - - -

JAPANESE LANTERNS IN many colors were strung over the dark lawn, defining a patch of light and movement behind the Clive mansion. A number of guests dressed in elegant informality clustered together inside the circling lanterns near a bar set up on a table with a white tablecloth, where a black man in a white coat made drinks upon request. I was there wearing a summer-weight blue blazer to hide my gun, and sipping some beer and eating an occasional mushroom turnover offered me by a black woman with cornrows, wearing a frilly white apron. If you went outside the lanterns into the surrounding darkness and waited until your eyes adjusted, you could look up and see stars in the velvety night.

Walter Clive was there in a straw-colored jacket and a navy-blue shirt. He still had on his aviator sunglasses, probably protection from the glare of the lanterns. A woman in a soft-green linen dress came out of the house and into the circle of light. She had silvery blond hair, and very worthwhile cleavage, and good hips and long legs. She was standing with a graceful-looking younger man with hair as blond as hers.

"Dolly," Clive said. "Over here."

She turned toward his voice and smiled and walked toward us. She had the kind of walk that helped me to think about the soft sound of the linen dress whispering across her thighs. When she got to where we were she kissed Clive, and put her hand out to me.

"Dolly, this is Spenser, the man we've hired."

"How lovely to meet you," she said.

Her grip was firm. She smelled gently of French perfume. At least in the light of the Japanese lanterns, her eyes were violet.

"How do you do?" I said.

"Have you met Hugger yet?"

"No, is he here?"

"Oh, aren't you funny," she said.

There was intimacy in the way Dolly stood and talked, which seemed to suggest that we really ought to be in bed together, and until then we were just marking time.

"Yes, I am," I said. "Do you have any theories on the horse assaults?"

"Oh Lord no," she said. "That's not my business."

"What is your business?" I said.

She nodded at Clive, who was talking with a group of guests.

"Keeping him happy," she said.

"Which you do well."

She didn't appear to do anything, but I could feel the energy between us again.

"Which I do *very* well," she said.

Penny came by and took my arm.

"Sorry, Dolly, the big boss has ordered me to introduce him around."

"It's best to follow orders," Dolly said, and drifted away toward Clive.

"Wife?" I said.

"Girlfriend."

"Where's your mother?"

"Left years ago. She lives in San Francisco with a guitarist."

"You get along?" I said.

"With Dolly? Oh sure. She keeps Daddy happy and when Daddy's happy, everybody's happy."

"Who's the younger blond guy she's with?"

"That's her son," Penny said. "Jason."

"She's older than she looks," I said.

Penny smiled brilliantly.

"We all are," she said.

With her arm through mine she steered me through the guests. We stopped in front of a woman whose idea of easy informality appeared to be gold sling-back shoes with glass heels and a gauzy white dress. She was good-looking. Every woman at the party was good-looking. They all looked as if they had just stepped from the shower and doused themselves with lilac water and taken plenty of time getting ready for the party.

"This is my big sister," she said. "Stonie. Stonie, this

is Mr. Spenser, whom Daddy has hired to protect Hugger."

"Well," Stonie said, "you certainly have the build for it."

"You have a nice build too," I said.

"Why, aren't you just lovely to notice."

The man with her turned away from his conversation and put out a hand.

"Cord Wyatt," he said. "I'm the lucky husband of this lady."

He was taller than I am and slim, with the kind of loose build I associated with polo players. Since I had never seen a polo match, my association may not have been accurate. He had the tan and the perfect smile, and so did his wife. Everybody had it. If I were a skin cancer specialist, I'd move right down here.

"And this is my middle sister, SueSue."

It was getting monotonous. Blond hair, tan skin, white teeth. SueSue's dress was flowered.

"Wow," SueSue said.

"Wow?" I said.

"No one told me you were a hunk," SueSue said.

"Sadly," I said, "no one has told me that either."

"Well, you surely are," she said.

"He doesn't look like so much to me," a man said.

"My husband, Pud," SueSue said.

I put my hand out. Pud didn't take it. He appeared to be drunk. As I thought of it, maybe SueSue was drunk too. Which was too bad—it took a little something away from the "hunk" designation.

"Pud," I said, and took my hand back.

Pud looked like he might weigh 250, but it was weight that had collected on a frame designed to support maybe 210. He had the look of a college football player ten years out of shape. He was probably stud duck at the Rotary Club cookouts. I could have taken him while whistling the Michigan fight song and balancing a seal on my nose.

Pud said, "So, how you doing, Hunk?"

"Fine, thank you, Pud."

I maybe put a little more edge into "Pud" than I had to, but on the whole I was being the soul of civility.

"My wife thinks you're a hunk," he said.

His tongue was having a little trouble, and "you're" came out as a compromise with "you are."

"A common misperception," I said. "You must have the same problem, Pud."

He frowned at me. Even sober, I suspected, his strong suit would not be thinking.

"You got yourself a problem," he said, "with my name?"

"Oh, Pud," SueSue said. "Nobody gives a damn about your silly old name."

Penny was quiet; she seemed sort of interested.

"The hunk don't like my name," he said, and stared at me. The stare would have been scarier if he could focus.

"It's quite a lovely name," I said. "Is it short for something?"

"His father's name was Poole," SueSue said. "Poole Potter. He called his son Puddle."

"I see," I said.

"I don't think I like you talking to my wife, Hunk."

"Of course you don't," I said.

"So buzz off."

He put his hand on my chest and gave me a little shove. It was too little. I didn't move.

"Pud," I said. "Please don't make a mistake here."

"Mistake? What mistake? I'm telling you to buzz off."

"You're drunk," I said, "and I'm even-tempered. But don't put your hands on me again."

He had a low-ball glass in his right hand that appeared to contain bourbon. He took a bracing pull on it.

"I ought to knock you on your keister."

"Sure," I said, "but you can't and you're just going to look like a goddamned fool. Why don't I apologize and you accept and we'll go our separate ways?"

"You think I can't?"

Neither Penny nor SueSue made any move to intervene. There was something a little unpleasant flickering in SueSue's eyes as she watched.

"Pud, I've been doing this for a living since before you started pickling your liver. It's not a good match for you."

He stared at me. Some part of him got it. Some part of him knew he'd gotten in where he didn't belong. But he was too drunk to back down. He looked at SueSue. The unpleasant glint was still in her eyes. She smiled an unpleasant smile.

"Don't you let him push you around, Pud Potter," she said.

He frowned as if he were trying to concentrate, and put his drink on a table next to him. It came the way I knew it would, a long slow looping right punch that I could have slipped while writing my memoirs. I blocked it on my left forearm. He threw a left of the same directness and velocity. I slipped the left, put my hand behind his shoulder, and used the slow force of the punch to continue him around. When he was turned, I put my foot against his butt and shoved. He stumbled forward and fell on the lawn, and got up with deep grass stains on the knees of his white slacks.

Walter Clive detached himself from the group he was entertaining and walked over. Dolly came with him.

"What seems to be the problem?" he said.

"Pud is drunk," Penny said.

Clive nodded. "And being Pud," he said.

"Yes."

Pud was standing, looking a little disoriented, ready to charge.

"SueSue," Clive said. "Take Pud home."

He turned to me.

"I apologize for my son-in-law. He's a little too fond sometimes of that sippin' whiskey."

"No harm," I said.

Clive never looked to see if Pud was leaving. Which he was, led by SueSue away from the bright circle of Japanese lanterns. Dolly smiled at me warmly. The smile made me think of perfumed silk. I was pretty sure I knew what she did to make Clive happy.

"Penny," Clive said, "introduce Mr. Spenser to our trainer."

"Sure thing, boss," Penny said, and put her arm through mine again and led me toward another part of the terrace. Clive went back to his guests with Dolly beside him.

"You handled him like he was a little boy," Penny said. She hugged my arm against her.

"It's what I do," I said. "As in most things, there's a pretty big difference between amateurs and professionals."

"I'll say."

"Sorry that had to happen," I said.

"Oh, not me," Penny said. "I'm thrilled. I think Pud needs to be kicked in the ass every evening."

"In your experience, am I going to have to do it again?"

"I don't know. He may not even remember it in the morning."

"Perhaps SueSue will remind him."

"You don't miss much," she said. "Do you?"

"Just doing my job, ma'am," I said.

"Most of the people Pud picks on are afraid of him."

"Given his fistic skills," I said, "he would be wise to ascertain that in advance."

She smiled and gave my arm an extra squeeze and guided me through the cocktail crowd.

FIVE

IT WAS TEN minutes to six in the morning. I was at the rail with Hale Martin, the Three Fillies trainer, at the east end of the Three Fillies training track with the sun on my back, drinking a cup of coffee from the pot in the trainer's room. A big chestnut horse was being ridden around the soft track by a small girl in jeans and a lavender T-shirt that read *THREE FILLIES* on it. A whip was stuck into the top of her right boot. Under her funny-looking rider's cap, her hair was a long single braid down her back. The girl was an exercise rider named Mickey. The horse was Hugger Mugger. He was beautiful. There were four other horses being galloped in the morning. They were beautiful. As I went along I discovered that they were all beautiful, including the ones that couldn't outrun me in a mile and a furlong. Maybe beauty is skin-deep.

"How much does he weigh?" I said.

"About twelve hundred pounds," Martin said.

I'd always imagined that trainers were old guys that looked like James Whitmore, and chewed plug tobacco. Martin was a young guy with even features and very bright blue eyes and the healthy color of a man who spent his life outdoors. He wore a white button-down shirt and pressed jeans, a silk tweed jacket, riding boots, and the kind of snug leather pullover chaps that horse people wore, I think, to indicate that they were horse people.

"And that hundred-pound kid controls him like he was a tricycle."

Martin smiled. "Girls and horses," he said.

"It's probably a sign of city-bred boorishness," I said. "But all the horses look pretty much alike."

"They ought to," Martin said. "They're all descended from one of three horses, most of them from a horse called the Darley Arabian."

"Close breeding," I said.

"Um-hmm."

We were alone at the rail except for the Security South guards in their gray uniforms, four of them, with handguns and walkie-talkies, watching Hugger Mugger as he pranced through his workout.

"Doesn't it make some of them kind of weird?"

"Oh yes," Martin said. "Weavers. Cribbers. Stay around until we breeze Jimbo. We can't breeze Jimbo with the other horses."

The stables and training track were surrounded by tall pine trees that didn't begin to branch until maybe thirty feet up the trunk. The horses' hooves made a soft chuff on the surface of the track. Otherwise it was very still. The exercise riders talked among themselves as they rode, but we weren't close enough to hear them. There was nothing else in sight but this ring in the trees where the horses circled timelessly, counterclockwise, with an evanescence of morning mist barely lingering about the infield.

"What's going on with that one?" I said.

"He tends to swallow his tongue," Martin said. "So we have to tie it down when he runs."

"How's he feel about that?" I said.

Martin grinned. "Horses don't say much."

"Nothing wrong with quiet," I said.

A trim man with short hair and high cheekbones came toward us from the stable area. He had on a tan golf jacket, and Dockers and deck shoes. A blue-and-gray-plaid shirt showed at the opening of the half-zipped jacket. He wore an earpiece like the Secret Service guys, and there was a small *SS* pin on the lapel of his jacket. When he got close enough I could see that he was wearing a gun under the golf jacket.

"Delroy," he said.

"Spenser," I said, trying to stand a little straighter.

"I heard you were coming aboard."

"Aye," I said.

Delroy looked at me suspiciously. Was I kidding him?

"I'd appreciate it if you'd check in with me when you're in the area."

"Sure. When did you come aboard?"

"Me?"

"Yeah, when did you start guarding the horses?"

"After Heroic Hope was shot."

"The second horse shot."

"That's right."

"So where were your guys when someone was pointing a gun at Hugger Mugger?"

"If somebody did," Delroy said.

"You figure the groom made it up?"

"Nobody could get to him through our security."

"How about the other horse, Saddle Shoes?"

"He was shot at long range," Delroy said. "We can't be everywhere."

"'Course not," I said. "Why would the groom lie?"

"Most of them lie," Delroy said.

"Grooms?"

Delroy snorted. "They wouldn't tell a white man the truth if it would make them rich."

"What's the *SS* for on your collar?"

"Security South."

"Oh, it's not *Schutzstaffel*?" I said.

"Excuse me?"

"A little Nazi humor," I said.

"What do you mean?"

"The SS was Hitler's bodyguard," I said. "It's an abbreviation of *Schutzstaffel*."

"This pin stands for Security South," Delroy said.

"Yes."

Delroy looked at me for a moment. Martin was silent beside me, his eyes on the horses moving around the track.

"You're a big guy," Delroy said.

"I try," I said.

"Well, to be honest with you, size doesn't impress me."

"How disappointing," I said.

"We're professionals, every one of us, and quite frankly, we don't think we need some wizard brought in here from Boston to tell us how to do our job."

"Well, it's certainly a nice professional-looking earpiece," I said. "Can you listen to Dr. Laura on it?"

"I command a twelve-man detail here," Delroy said. "I need in-touch capability."

"Military Police?" I said.

"I joined SS five years ago. Before that I was with the Bureau and before that I was an officer in the Marine Corps."

"The Corps and the Bureau," I said. "Jeepers."

"What are your credentials?"

"I got fired from the cops," I said.

Delroy snorted. Martin kept watching the horses.

"How the hell did you weasel onto Walt Clive's payroll?" Delroy said.

"Maybe size impresses him," I said.

"Well, let's put it on the table where we can all look at it," Delroy said. "We'll complete our mission here with you or without you. You do whatever you want to, or whatever Walt Clive wants you to do. But if you get in our way we'll roll right over you. You understand?"

"Most of it," I said. "Martin here can help me with the hard parts."

"Anything has to do with that horse," Delroy said, "you go through me."

He about-faced smartly and marched away.

"First Pud, now him," I said to Martin.

"Southern hospitality," Martin said absently. His mind was still on the horses.

"Just so we're clear," I said. "I'm not after your wife. I won't tell you how to train horses."

"My wife will be sorry to hear that," Martin said.

"But the horses won't give a damn," I said.

"They never seem to," Martin said.

SIX

I WAS SITTING in an office at the Columbia County Sheriff's Lamarr substation with a man named Dalton Becker. He was a big, solid, slow black man. He had short graying hair. His coat was off and hanging behind the half-open door. His red-and-blue-striped suspenders were bright over his white shirt. He wore his gun tucked inside his waistband.

"You care for a Coca-Cola?" he said.

"Sure."

"Vonnie." He raised his voice. "Couple Coca-Colas."

We waited while a young black woman with bright blond hair sashayed in, chewing gum, and plopped two Cokes on his desk.

"Thank you, Vonnie," Becker said.

She sashayed back out. He handed one to me, opened his, and took a drink.

"Here's what I know about this horse business," he

said. "First of all, there's been three horses attacked. Not counting the alleged attack on Hugger Mugger. One of them died. All three attacks were here at Three Fillies. Far's I know, there have been no other attacks on other horses."

"Alleged?"

"Yep. We only got the groom's word."

"You believe the groom?" I said.

"I been at this awhile. I don't believe or not believe. I just look for evidence."

"Anything wrong with the groom?"

"Nope."

"Just native skepticism," I said.

"You got any of that?"

"Some," I said.

Becker smiled. I waited.

"First one was about a month ago, at the training track, here in Lamarr. Stable pony got plugged with a .22 caliber slug. Bullet went into the brain through the eye socket. He died. You know what a stable pony is?"

"I know he's not a racehorse."

"That's enough to know," Becker said. "I don't know squat about horse racing either."

"The other two were Thoroughbreds, one shot from a distance, probably a rifle with a scope, while he was walking around the training track. Hit him in the neck. I guess he'll recover. The other one was shot in the shoulder—he's all right, but I guess his racing days are finished. Both bullets were .22 long."

As we talked Becker sipped on his Coke; otherwise

he didn't move at all. He wasn't inert, he was solid. It was as if he would move when he chose to and nothing would move him before.

"Same weapon in all the shootings?"

"Far as anybody can tell," Becker said.

"One bullet each?"

"Yep."

"Is there a case file?" I said.

"Sure. Why?"

"Just wondered if you bothered," I said.

"Always had a good memory," Becker said. "You can look at the file, if you want to."

"Suspects?" I said.

"Well, so far I'm pretty sure it ain't me," Becker said.

"Think it's the same person?"

"Could be. Or it could be one person shot the first one and a copycat shot the others. They're always out there. Could be somebody with a grudge against Clive."

"Any evidence that it's either?"

"Nope," Becker said. "No evidence for anything."

"Sort of up the Swanee without a paddle," I said.

"Till you showed up. Nothing makes us dumb southern boys happier than having a smart Yankee show up to help us."

"You going to break out in a rebel yell soon?" I said.

"Well," Becker said, "I do get playful sometimes."

"I thought you were supposed to be ticked off about slavery and stuff."

"Never been a slave. Don't know anybody who owned one."

"Any pattern to the wounds?" I said.

"Veterinary report's in the case file," Becker said. "To me they look random."

"So why would somebody go around randomly shooting horses?"

"Don't know."

"The shots were random," I said, "but the horses weren't. They all belonged to Three Fillies."

"Yep."

"Try not to run on so," I said. "You're making me dizzy."

Becker smiled.

"If you wanted a dead horse, wouldn't you shoot more than once? Especially if the horse didn't go down?"

"If I had time," Becker said. "If I wanted a dead horse. Might use a bigger weapon too."

"Did he have time?"

"Far as we know."

"And there are probably bigger weapons available."

"Yep."

"So maybe a dead horse wasn't the point," I said.

"Maybe."

"Maybe shooting the horse was the point."

"Maybe."

"If he wanted to prevent them from racing for some reason, why shoot the pony?"

"Good question," Becker said.

"So why'd he shoot them?"

"Maybe he's a fruitcake," Becker said.

"Maybe," I said. "You familiar with Security South?"

"Sure," Becker said. "Bunch of ex-FBI guys. Do a lot of horse-racing security."

"Know a guy named Delroy?"

"Jon Delroy," Becker said.

"Brisk, stern, upright, and ready," I said.

"You bet," Becker said. "Awful dumb, though."

SEVEN

I WAS IN the Three Fillies stable yard looking at Hugger Mugger. Security South had a guy with a gleaming pistol belt posted in front of the stall and another one in the stable office making sure of the coffee. Hugger Mugger hung his head out of the stall and looked hopefully at Penny in case she might have a carrot. He had very large brown eyes and looked deeply intelligent.

"They're not terribly smart," Penny said. "They seem to have a lot of certain kinds of awareness people don't have. They are very skittish and can be spooked by dogs, or birds, or sudden noise."

Hugger Mugger nosed her upper arm, his ears back slightly and his profound brown eyes gazing at her. Along the stable row other horses looked out over the open doors of their stalls, turning their heads to peer down at us. The horses were restrained only by a belt across the open door. It was not unlike the velvet rope that closes off a dining room.

"Does he know you?" I said.

"He knows I sometimes carry carrots," Penny said. "Mostly they like other horses."

"They ever get to gallop around in the field with all the other horses?"

"God no," Penny said. "You pay two million dollars for a horse that might be the next Citation, you can't let him hang around with other horses, one of which might kick his ribs in."

I patted Hugger Mugger's forehead. He turned the carrot-questioning look on me.

"Nice horsie," I said.

"Aficionados of the sport of kings," Penny said, "don't usually say things like 'nice horsie.' "

I frowned and looked hard at Hugger Mugger. In a deep voice I said, "Good withers."

Penny laughed. "Do you even know what withers are?" she said.

"No," I said.

"You talk with Billy?" she said.

"I will."

"You'll like him."

"I never met a man I didn't like," I said.

Penny gave me an *Oh please* look. "He loves this horse," she said.

"Because he's going to win the Triple Crown?" I said.

"No. That's why all the rest of us love him. I think Billy just loves him."

"Even if he doesn't win the Triple Crown?"

"Even if he never wins a race."

"Love is not love which alters when it alteration finds," I said.

"Is that some kind of poem?" Penny said.

"I think so."

"You don't look like a poem kind of man," she said.

"It's a disguise," I said.

Jon Delroy came briskly toward us across the stable yard.

"I got a message you wanted to see me," he said to Penny.

"Yes, Jon," she said. "Let's the three of us go over to the office."

Delroy looked at me as if I were something he'd just stepped in. And turned to walk with Penny. I tagged along. We went into the track office and sat down. Penny sat behind the desk in a swivel chair. Delroy and I sat in straight chairs against the wall. There was a coffeemaker on a table near the desk, and a small refrigerator on the wall behind the desk. There were photographs of happy owners with happy jockeys and happy horses in various winner's circles.

"Jon, you've lodged a complaint with Three Fillies Stables," Penny said. "About Mr. Spenser."

She sat back in the swivel chair, her feet in riding boots crossed on the desk. Her voice was friendly, with the nice southern lilt.

"I've talked with your father, yes," Delroy said.

"And my father has asked me to talk with both of you," she said.

I waited. Delroy was looking hard at her, sitting bolt upright in his chair.

"As CEO of, and majority stockholder in, Three Fillies Stables, my father feels that employment decisions are his to make if he wishes to."

"Well, of course, Penny, but . . ."

"Don't interrupt," Penny said. No lilt. "We have hired Spenser to find out who is trying to harm Hugger Mugger. We have hired you to protect Hugger Mugger while he does so. There is no reason for either of you to get in the other's way."

I smiled cooperatively. Delroy looked as if he had just eaten a pinecone.

"Is that clear?" Penny said.

"Yes, ma'am," I said.

Delroy didn't speak.

"Is that clear, Jon?"

Delroy still didn't speak.

"Because if it is not clear, you may finish out the week and then be on your way."

"Penny, we signed a contract."

"Sue us. This is my way or the highway, Jon. And you decide right now."

"Be easier to put up with me," I said to Delroy.

Penny sat with her feet still up on the desk. Her big pretty eyes showed nothing. She wore a white shirt, with the collar open, a gold chain showing. Her pale blue jeans were tight and tucked into the top of her riding boots. Her neck was slender but strong-looking. Her thighs were firm.

"Yes or no," she said.

"Yes," Delroy said.

The word came out very thin, as if it'd had to slip between clenched teeth.

"You'll cooperate with Spenser?"

"Yes."

"You have any problems with Jon?" Penny said to me.

"Not me," I said. "Your way or the doorway."

Penny took her feet off the desktop and let the chair come forward and smiled.

"Excellent," she said. "Either of you want a Coca-Cola?"

EIGHT

- - - - - - - - - - - - - - - - -

MY ROOM WAS on the second floor of one wing of the motel, and opened onto a wing-length balcony with stairs at either end. It was late afternoon when SueSue Potter knocked on my door.

"Welcome Wagon," she said when I opened it.

"Oh good," I said. "I was afraid your husband had sent you ahead to soften me up."

She was wearing a big hat and carrying a bottle of champagne in an ice bucket and a big straw handbag. There was some sort of look in her eyes, but it wasn't the unpleasant glint I'd seen when Pud threatened me.

"Oh, Pud is a poop," she said.

"Alliteration," I said. "Very nice."

She put the champagne down on top of the television set and circled the room. She was as perky as a grasshopper and much better-looking in a pink linen dress with a square neck and matching shoes.

"You mean you have to live here all by yourself all the time you're here?" she said.

"Depends on how lucky I get hanging out at the bowling alley late."

"You big silly, I bet you don't even bowl."

"Wow," I said, "you see right through a guy."

"You have any glasses for this champagne?"

"Couple of nice plastic ones," I said, "in the bathroom."

"Well, get them out here, it's nearly cocktail time and I don't like to enter it sober."

I went to the bathroom and got the two little cups and peeled off the plastic-wrap sealers and brought the cups out and set them festively on top of the television beside the champagne bucket.

"I'm afraid that champagne corks are just too strong for me. Could you very kindly do the honors?"

I opened the champagne and poured some into each of the plastic cups. I handed one to her and picked up the other one. She put her glass up toward mine.

"Chink, chink," she said.

I touched her glass with mine.

"I think plastic sounds more like 'Scrape, scrape,' " I said.

"Not if you listen with a romantic ear," she said.

"Which you do," I said.

"To everything, darlin'."

I smiled. She smiled. She drank her champagne. I took another small nibble at mine. She gazed dreamily around the room. I waited. She looked at my gun, lying in its holster on the bedside table.

"Oh," she said. "A gun."

"Why, so it is."

"Can I look at it?"

"Sure."

"Can I pick it up?"

"No."

She put her glass out. I refilled it.

"Did you have that with you the other night when Pud was being dreadful?"

"Yes."

"So you could have shot him if you wanted."

"Seems a little extreme," I said.

"You handled him like he was a bad little boy," Sue-Sue said.

She drank some more champagne, looking at me while she drank, her eyes big and blue and full of energy. It was too soon for the champagne to kick in. It was some other kind of energy.

"Just doing my job, ma'am."

She smiled widely. And what I'd seen in her eyes, I saw in her smile.

"Pud played football over at Alabama. Even had a pro tryout."

"Linebacker?" I said.

"I don't know who the pro team was. I hate football."

"What position did he play?" I said.

"Defense."

I nodded.

"He still goes to the gym all the time. But you just turned him around like he was a little bitty boy."

"Breathtaking, isn't it?" I said.

"You're a dangerous man," she said, and put her glass out. I poured.

"Especially to fried clams," I said. "You put a plate of fried clams in front of me, they're gone in a heart-beat."

"I could see that you were dangerous," she said, "minute you came into the room."

The champagne was beginning to affect her speech a little. Her articles were slurring, or she was skipping right over them.

"I think even Pud could see it, but he was too drunk to be smart about it. What would you have done if he'd come back at you?"

"You kind of have to be in the moment," I said, "to know what you'd do."

"You'd have hurt him," SueSue said. "I saw it in your eyes."

"I take no pleasure in hurting someone."

"I know men, darlin'. Everybody else in my damn family knows horses. But I know men. You like to fight."

"Everybody needs a hobby," I said.

"You like to fuck too?"

"Wow," I said. "You do know men."

A little vertical frown line indented her perfect tan for a moment, between her perfect eyebrows, and went right away.

"Lotta men don't like it. They all pretend they like it, but they don't. Some of them don't want to, or they can't 'cause they a little teensy bit drunk, or they scared of a woman who wants to."

"And you're a woman who wants to."

"I like it. I like it with big men. I'd like to see how many muscles you got and where."

"Lots," I said. "Everywhere."

"I need to see for myself, darlin'."

"That'll be a problem."

"You aren't even drinking your champagne," she said. "If you don't like champagne, I got something more serious."

"No need," I said.

But SueSue wasn't all that interested in my needs.

"You married?" Sue said.

"Sort of."

"You don't wear a wedding band."

"I'm not exactly married."

"How can you be not exactly married?" she said. "You mean you got a girlfriend."

"More than that," I said.

"Good Lord, you're not gay, are you?"

"No."

"Well, whatever it is, you being loyal about it?"

"Yes."

"Oh hell," she said.

I nodded.

"Cheatin' makes it a lot more fun, darlin'," she said.

Her southern accent became more pronounced as the champagne bubbled into her system.

"Maybe it's not always about fun," I said.

"Well, what in the hell else would it be about?"

"Could be about love," I said.

"Love?" She laughed. The sound was unpleasant.

"Only some big dangerous gun-totin' Yankee would come around talking 'bout love. My God—love!"

"I heard it makes the world go round," I said.

"Money makes the world go round, darlin'. And sex makes the trip worthwhile. Sex and money, darlin'. Money and sex."

"Both are nice," I said.

She picked up the champagne bottle. It was empty. She put it back onto the table.

"Damn," she said, and half disappeared into her big straw handbag and came out with a bottle of Jack Daniel's. She handed it to me to open.

"Nice." She laughed the unpleasant laugh again. "There isn't anything nice down here, darlin'. Nothing nice about the Clives."

I put the open bottle of Jack Daniel's on the table beside the champagne bucket. SueSue took some ice out of the bucket and put it in the cup from which she had been drinking champagne. She picked up the Jack Daniel's bottle and poured some over the rocks. Holding the bottle, she looked at me. I shook my head. The champagne left in my plastic cup was warm. I put the cup down on the table.

"Nothing?" I said.

SueSue drank some Jack Daniel's. She neither sipped it nor slugged it. She drank it as she had drunk champagne, in an accomplished manner, doing something she was used to doing.

"Well," she said, "we're all good-looking, and mostly we have good manners, 'cept me. I tend maybe to be a little bit too direct for good manners."

"Direct," I said, and smiled at her hunkishly. "What's wrong with your family?"

"The hell with them," she said. "Are you going to come on to me or not?"

"Let's talk a little," I said.

She got cagey. "Only if you'll have little drink with me," she said.

I wanted to hear what she had to say. I picked up my cup and took it to the bathroom and emptied the remaining champagne into the sink. Then I came back, put some ice in my plastic cup and poured some whiskey over it.

"Now drink some," SueSue said.

I felt like a freshman girl on her first date with a senior. We drank together in silence for a minute or so. I was betting that SueSue couldn't tolerate silence. I was right.

"What was it you were asking me about, darlin'?"

"You," I said. "Tell me about you."

More than one way to ask a question.

"I'm a Clive," she said.

"Is that complicated?"

She shook her head sadly.

"I think one of our ancestors must have stolen something from a tomb," she said.

"Family curse?"

"We're all corrupt," she said. "Drunks, liars, fornicators."

"You too?" I said.

"Me especially," she said. "Hell, why do you think I'm married to Fred Flintstone?"

"Love?" I said.

She made a nasty sound, which might have been a contemptuous laugh.

"There you go again," she said. "Daddy wanted his girls married. He wanted them out of the clubs and off their backs and in a marriage. He wanted sons-in-law to inherit the business. Pud was what there was."

"Stonie too?"

"Don't get me started on Stonie and Cord."

"Why not?"

"Don't get me started," she said.

"Okay."

SueSue had a drink of whiskey.

"How about Penny?" I said. "She's not married."

"Little Penelope," SueSue said. She struggled to say "Penelope." "Sometimes I think she was switched at birth."

"She's different?"

"She stands up to Daddy."

"And?"

"And he thinks it's cute. He trusts her with everything. Hell, she knows the business better than he does."

"So she doesn't have to get married?"

"Not now, but she better, she wants to inherit anything."

"Really?"

"Man's gotta be in charge," SueSue said. "Can't have a woman ruining the business."

"Even though she halfway runs it now."

"Daddy still in charge."

Talking was getting harder for her as the Jack

Daniel's went in. I needed to get what I could before talking became too hard.

"What's wrong with Stonie and Cord?" I said.

"Stonie so frustrated she rubbing up doorknobs," SueSue said.

Her syntax was deteriorating fast.

"How come?"

Her smile was dreamy without ceasing to be nasty.

"Little boys," she said.

"Cord likes little boys?" I said.

Her eyes closed and her head lolled back against the chair cushion.

She said, "Un-huh."

And then she fell asleep.

NINE

I WAS HAVING breakfast with Billy Rice off the back of a commissary truck parked under some high pines at the edge of the Three Fillies training track.

"Donuts put a nice foundation under your morning," Rice said.

"Go good with coffee too," I said.

Across from us the track was empty, except for Hugger Mugger. We could hear him breathing in the short heavy way that horses breathe. His chest was huge. His legs were positively dainty, the odd, beautiful result of endless selectivity. A half-ton heart-lung machine on legs smaller than mine. His only function was to run a mile or so, in two minutes or so. Rice watched him all the time while we ate our donuts.

"Great horse?" I said.

"Be a great horse," Rice said.

"Doesn't look that different."

"Ain't what makes a great horse," Billy said. "Same

as any athlete. He got to have the right body, and the right training. Then he got to have the heart. One with the heart be the great one."

"And he's got it?"

"Yes, he do."

"How do you know?"

Rice was too gentle a man to be scornful. But he came close.

"I know him," Rice said.

He was smallish. Not smallish like a jockey, just smallish compared to me. He wore jeans and sneakers and a polo shirt and a baseball cap that read *THREE FILLIES* across the front, over the bill. Martin, the trainer, leaned on the fence watching Hugger Mugger. And four Security South sentinels stood around the track.

"Tell me about the prowler," I said.

Rice sipped his coffee. His dark eyes were thoughtful and opaque, a little like the eyes of the racehorses.

"Nothing much to tell. I sleeping with Hugger. I hear a noise, shine my flashlight, see a gun. When I shine my light, the gun goes away. I hear footsteps running. Then nothing."

"You didn't follow?"

"I don't have no gun. Am I going out in the dark, chase somebody got a gun?"

"No," I said. "You're not."

"How 'bout you?" Rice said.

"I'm not either," I said. "Can you describe the gun?"

"No. Don't know much 'bout guns."

"Handgun or long gun?"

"Long gun."

"Shotgun or rifle?"

"Don't know."

"One barrel or two?"

"One."

"What kind of front sight?"

"Don't know," Rice said. "Only saw it in the flash-light for a second."

"Color?"

"Color? What color is a gun barrel? It was iron-colored."

"Bluish?"

"Yes, I guess."

"How about the footsteps? Heavy? Light? Fast? Slow?"

"Just footsteps, sounded like running. It was on the dirt outside the stable. Didn't make a lot of noise."

"Any smells?"

"Smells?"

"Hair tonic, shaving lotion, cologne, perfume, mouthwash, tobacco, booze, liniment."

"Sleeping in the stable," Rice said, "mostly everything smells like horses."

I nodded.

"They going to bring Jimbo out," Rice said. "Time to get Hugger out the way."

The exercise rider brought Hugger Mugger to the rail. Billy snapped the lead shank onto his bridle. The exercise rider climbed down, and Billy led Hugger Mugger back toward the stable area. As they walked their heads were very close together, as if they were exchanging confidences. The security guards moved in closer around Hugger Mugger as he walked, and by the time he'd reached the stable area they were around him like the Secret Service.

I moved up beside Hale Martin. Coming from the stable area toward the track was an entourage of horses and horse keepers. There was a big chestnut horse with a rider up and a groom on either side holding a shank. With them were two other horsemen, one on each side. The chestnut was tossing his head and skittering sideways as he came.

"Jimbo?" I said to Martin.

"Jimbo," Martin said.

The outriders gave with him as Jimbo skittered, and closed back in on him when he stopped. Riding him was a red-haired girl who might have been seventeen. The grooms and the outriders were men. One of the outriders had a cast on his right leg. He rode to the right, so that the injured leg was away from Jimbo.

"What about the guy with the cast?" I said.

Martin grinned.

"Jimbo," he said.

When Jimbo was on the track, the outriders peeled off and sat their horses in the shade near the track entrance. The grooms unsnapped their lead shanks at the same time and stepped quickly away. Jimbo reared and made horse noises. The red-haired girl held his head straight, sitting high up on his shoulders as if she were part of the horse. She gave him a light tap on the backside with her whip, and Jimbo tossed his head and began to move down the track.

"Run him a lot," I said. "Get him tired."

"Just makes him cranky," Martin said, his eyes following Jimbo. The redhead let him out and he began to sprint.

"Has he killed anyone yet?"

"Nope."

"But he might," I said.

"He wants to," Martin said.

"You have to handle him like this all the time?"

"Yep."

"Is it worth the bother?"

"He can run," Martin said.

"How about gelding?"

"Somebody gelded John Henry," Martin said. "Do you know how much money that cost them?"

"Stud fees?"

"You bet."

"You mean you'd let Jimbo loose with a mare?"

"He's different around mares," Martin said.

"Him too," I said.

TEN

MICKEY BLAIR WENT out of the track office with a springy walk that made her long blond braid bounce against the full length of her spine. She left the door open behind her. Through the open door, I could look straight along the stable row where the horses hung their heads out of their stalls and looked around. It reminded me of one of those streets in Amsterdam where the whores sat in windows.

I had a yellow legal-size pad on the desk by my right hand, and a nice Bic pen lying on it at a rakish angle. The pad was blank. I had spent the day interviewing stable crew about the attempt on Hugger Mugger and had learned so little that I thought I might have crossed into deficit. I looked at my watch. Twenty to five. Penny Clive came in wearing black jeans and a white T-shirt and a black jacket. She went to the refrigerator, took out two Cokes, and handed me one. She sat down on the couch and put her feet up on the coffee table. I was able to observe that her jeans fit her very well. It was about the only thing I'd observed all day.

"You got him in your sights?" she said.

"I think I know somewhat less than I did this morning."

"Oh dear," Penny said.

We each drank some Coke.

"I gather my sister came to visit," Penny said.

"Where did you gather that?" I said.

She smiled and shrugged.

"Daddy likes to know what SueSue and Stonie are up to," she said.

"So you keep an eye on them?"

"It's a small community," Penny said. "I usually know what's going on in it."

"Someone at the motel tipped you."

She smiled.

"Because you'd alerted them," I said.

She continued to smile.

"Because you figured she'd come to call," I said.

"SueSue is predictable," Penny said.

"Who keeps an eye on *you*?" I said.

"I'm self-regulating," Penny said, and her smile increased so that the laugh parentheses at the corners of her mouth deepened. "I hope SueSue wasn't offensive."

"Not at all," I said.

"She has a problem with alcohol," Penny said.

"I gathered that she might."

"And men," Penny said.

I was quiet. Penny was quiet.

Finally Penny said, "Did she come on to you?"

"I wondered how you were going to get to it. Straight on is good."

"Thank you. Did she?"

"I think that's between SueSue and me," I said.

Penny nodded.

"Of course," she said. "I'm sorry to be cross-examining you."

"Just doing your job," I said.

"It's not like it sounds," she said. "My sisters are both, what, wild? Daddy is just trying . . . He's being a daddy."

"How are the marriages?" I said.

"They don't work very well."

"Children?"

"No."

"How's Daddy feel about that?"

"He wants an heir."

"Is it up to you?" I said.

She almost blushed.

"Not yet, not now," she said. "I've got too much to do here. Three Fillies is a huge operation, Daddy can't run it by himself anymore."

"Gee, he looks fine," I said.

"Oh, he is. But he's got too much money now. He's . . . too important. He travels a great deal now. He and Dolly. He just can't concentrate anymore on the day-to-day grind of it."

"How about the sons-in-law?" I said.

She shrugged. "They're married to his daughters," Penny said.

"Isn't Cord the executive VP?"

"Yes."

"And Pud is . . . ?"

"VP for marketing."

"Are they real jobs?" I said.

"Well, you come straight at it too, don't you?"

"Susan does subtle," I said. "I'm not smart enough."

"Of course you're not," Penny said. "No, they aren't real jobs. I think Daddy hoped they would be. But Pud is . . . well, you saw Pud."

"I saw him at his worst," I said.

"True, and he's not always that bad. When he's sober he's kind of a good old boy."

"When is he sober?"

"Almost every day," Penny said, "until lunch."

"And Stonie's husband?"

"Cord."

I nodded. She looked out at the line of stalls. Hugger Mugger, third from the end, was looking out of his stall past the Security South guard as if he were pondering eternity.

"You think he's pondering eternity?" I said.

"Hugger? He's pondering lunch," Penny said.

"How about Cord?" I said. "Is he a good old boy, when he's sober?"

She looked almost startled.

"No, Cord isn't a drinker," she said. "A little white wine to be social, maybe."

"And as an executive VP?"

She shook her head. "Cord's very artistic."

"So was Wallace Stevens," I said.

"Isn't he some kind of poet?"

"Yes. He was also vice president of an insurance company."

"Isn't that odd," Penny said. "Cord isn't really interested in business, I'm afraid."

"What's he interested in?"

"Are you being a detective again?"

"I'm always being a detective," I said.

"Why do you want to know about Cord?"

"Because I don't know. Part of what I do is collect information. When I have collected enough I sometimes know something."

"Well, I think it's time to stop talking about my family."

"Sure," I said.

We were quiet for a while.

"I know I introduced the topic," Penny said.

I nodded. Penny smiled. Her teeth were very white against her honeyed tan.

"So I guess I can unintroduce it," she said.

"Sure," I said.

"I don't want you to think ill of us," Penny said. "All families have their problems. But all in all, we're a pretty nice group."

I didn't know what all this had to do with Hugger Mugger. But I was used to not knowing. I expected sooner or later that I would know. For now I simply registered that she hadn't wanted to talk about Cord and Stonie. I decided not to mention what SueSue had told me.

"Of course you are," I said.

ELEVEN

I SAT WITH Walter Clive at the Three Fillies syndication office in downtown Lamarr. He wore some sort of beige woven-silk pullover, tan linen slacks, no socks, and burgundy loafers. His tan remained golden. His silver hair was brushed straight back. A thick gold chain showed at his neck. His nails were buffed. He was clean-shaven and smelled gently of cologne.

"Penny tells me you're making progress," Clive said.

He was leaning back in his high-backed red-leather swivel chair, with his fingers interlocked over his flat stomach. There was a wide gold wedding band on his left hand. Past the bay window behind him I could see the white flowers of some blossoming shrub.

"Penny exaggerates," I said.

"Really?" he said.

"I have made no progress that I can tell."

"Well, at least you're honest," Clive said.

"At least that," I said.

"Perhaps Penny simply meant that you had talked to a number of people."

"That's probably it," I said. "I have managed to annoy Jon Delroy."

"Penny mentioned that too."

"Thanks for having her talk with him."

"Actually that was Penny's doing."

"Well, it was effective."

"Jon's been with me a long time," Clive said. "He's probably feeling a little displaced."

"How long?"

"Oh, what, maybe ten years."

"Really. What was he doing?"

Clive paused, as if the conversation had gone off in a direction he hadn't foreseen.

"I have a large enterprise here. There is need for security."

"Sure. Well, he and I seem to be clear on our roles now."

Clive nodded, and leaned forward and pushed the button on an intercom.

"Marge," he said. "Could you bring us coffee."

A voice said that it would, and Clive leaned back again and smiled at me. The window to my right was partially open and I could hear desultory birdsong in the flowering trees.

"So," Clive said, "have you reached a conclusion of any sort?"

"Other than I'm not making any progress?" I said.

"Yes," Clive said. "Are you for instance formulating any theories?"

"I've mostly observed that this thing doesn't make any sense," I said.

"Well, it is, sort of by definition," Clive said, "a series of senseless crimes."

"Seems so," I said.

"Meaning?"

"Meaning it seems so senseless that maybe it isn't."

Clive hadn't become a tycoon by nodding in agreement to everything said.

"That sounds like one of those clever statements people make when they're trying to sell you something you don't need," Clive said. "Does it mean anything?"

"I don't know," I said. "I can't say I know much about animal shootings. But for serial killers of people, you look for the logic that drives them. It's not necessarily other people's logic, but they are responding to some sort of interior pattern, and what you try to do is find it. The horse shootings are patternless."

"Or you haven't found it," Clive said.

"Or I haven't found it."

"They are all Three Fillies horses," Clive said. "Isn't that a pattern?"

"Maybe," I said. "But it is a pattern that leads us nowhere much. Why is someone shooting Three Fillies horses?"

"You're not supposed to be asking me," Clive said.

"I know," I said. "Is there anyone with a grudge against you?"

"Oh certainly. I can't name anyone in particular. But I've been in a tough business for more than thirty years. I'm bound to have made someone angry."

"Angry enough to shoot your horses?"

"Well, if they were, why would they shoot those horses? The stable pony's worth maybe five hundred dollars. Neither of the other two horses showed much promise. Heroic Hope can't run again, but insurance covers it. If you wish to damage me, you shoot Hugger Mugger—no amount of insurance could replace him."

"Me either," I said. "Maybe they were chosen because their loss would not be damaging."

"That doesn't make any sense."

"True," I said. "If someone didn't want to damage you they could just not shoot the horses."

A good-looking woman with close-cropped hair and high cheekbones and blue-black skin came in pushing a tea wagon. There was coffee in a silver decanter and white china cups and a cream and sugar set that matched the decanter. She served us each coffee and departed. I added cream and two lumps of sugar. Clive took his black.

"So what kind of security did Jon Delroy do for you?" I said.

"Why do you ask?" Clive said.

"Because I don't know."

"And you find that sufficient reason?" Clive said.

"Admittedly, I'm a nosy guy," I said. "It's probably one of the reasons I do what I do. But that aside, doing what I do is simply a matter of looking for the truth under a rock. It's under some rock, but I don't usually know which one. So whenever I come to a rock, I try to turn it over."

"Doesn't that sometimes mean you discover things you didn't need to know? Or want to know?"

"Yes."

"But you do it anyway?"

"I don't know how else to go about it," I said.

Clive looked at me heavily. He drank some coffee. Outside the window some birds fluttered about. They seemed to be sparrows, but they were moving too quickly to reveal themselves to me.

"I have three daughters," he said. "Two of whom have inherited their mother's depravity."

"Penny being the exception?" I said.

"Yes. They have not only indulged their depravity as girls, they have married badly, and marriage has appeared to exacerbate the depravity."

Clive wasn't looking at me. He wasn't, as far as I could tell, looking at anything. His eyes seemed blankly focused on the middle distance.

"Depravity loves company," I said.

I wasn't sure that Clive heard me. He continued to sit silently, looking at nothing.

"Among Delroy's duties was keeping tabs on the girls," I said.

He was silent still, and then slowly his eyes refocused on me.

"And dealing with the trouble they got into, and their husbands got into," he said.

"Such as?"

Clive shook his head. Outside, the birds had gone away and at the window there was only the flutter of the

curtains in the warm Georgia air. I put my empty coffee
cup on the tray and stood up.

"Thanks for the coffee," I said.

"You understand," he said.

"I do," I said.

TWELVE

– – – – – – – – – – – – – – –

Since it was evening, and I wasn't being feted at the Clive estate, I had the chance to lie on the bed in my motel and talk on the phone with Susan Silverman, whom I missed.

"So far," I said, "only one sister has made an active attempt to seduce me."

"How disappointing," Susan said. "Are there many sisters?"

"Three."

"Maybe the other two are just waiting until they know you better."

"Probably," I said.

"I have never found seducing you to be much of a challenge," Susan said.

"I try not to be aloof," I said.

We were silent for a moment. The air-conditioning hummed in the dim room. Outside, in the dark night, thick with insects, the full weight of the Georgia summer sat heavily.

"Are you making any progress professionally?" Susan said after a time.

"I'm getting to know my employer and his family."

"And?"

"And I may be in a Tennessee Williams play. . . . The old man seems sort of above the fray. He's separated, got a girlfriend, looks better than George Hamilton, and appears to leave the day-to-day management of the business to his youngest daughter."

"What's she like?"

"I like her. She's smart and centered. She finds me amusing."

"So even if she weren't smart and centered . . ." Susan said.

"Actually, that's how I know she's smart and centered," I said.

Susan's laugh across the thousand miles was immediate and intimate and as much of home as I was ever likely to have. It made my throat hurt.

"What about the other sisters?" Susan said.

I told her what I knew.

"You have any comment on a woman married to a man who prefers little boys?" I said.

"It would probably be preferable if she were married to a man who preferred her."

"Wow," I said. "You shrinks know stuff."

"In my practice, I know what my patients tell me. I know nothing about Stonie and whatsisname."

"Cord."

"Cord," she said. "And there is no one-fits-all template for a woman married to a man who prefers boys—if what SueSue told you is true."

"SueSue says that Stonie is so sexually frustrated that she is a threat to every doorknob," I said.

"Maybe she is," Susan said. "Or maybe that's just SueSue's projection of how she herself would be."

"And Cord? You figure he married her to get cover?" I said.

"Maybe," Susan said. "Or maybe he married her because he loves her."

"I could not love thee half so much, loved I not small boys more?"

"Sexuality is a little complicated."

"I've heard that," I said. "What bothers me in all of this is that I've got a series of so-far inexplicable crimes, committed in the midst of this family full of, I don't even know the right word for it—dippy?—people. I mean, there ought to be a connection but there isn't, or at least I can't find it."

"You'll find it if it's there," Susan said. "But most families are full of dippiness. Perhaps you don't always find yourself so fully in the bosom of a client's family, and thus don't have it shoved in your face from such close range."

"Maybe. Do you think there's a connection?"

"I have no way to know," Susan said.

"Do you think a man who prefers boys, or a woman who is married to a man who prefers boys, would have a reason to kill some horses?"

"As I've said, mine is a retrospective profession, as is

yours. We're much better at explaining why people did things than we are at predicting what they might do."

"Our business is generally after the fact," I said.

"Yes."

"You're not going to solve this for me, then."

"No. I'm not."

"And what about my sexual needs?"

"I could talk dirty on the phone."

"I think I'm too old for that to work anymore," I said.

"Then unless you're coming home soon, I guess you'll have to mend your fences with SueSue."

"And if I do?"

"I'll shoot her, and swear I was aiming at a horse."

"I thought you shrinks had too much self-control for jealousy," I said.

"Only during office hours."

THIRTEEN

- - - - - - - - - - - - - - - - - - -

I WAS JUST finished shaving when I got a call from Becker, the Lamarr sheriff's deputy.

"Got a horse shot over in Alton, in South Carolina. Thought I'd drive over and have a look. You want to ride along?"

"Yes."

"Pick you up in 'bout fifteen minutes."

I was standing in front of the motel by the lobby door when Becker pulled up in a black Ford Crown Victoria. There was a blue light sitting on the dashboard, and a long buggy whip antenna, but no police markings. When I got in, the car smelled of food. Becker was drinking coffee. On the seat beside him was a large brown paper bag.

"Got us some sausage biscuits," Becker said, "and coffee. Help yourself."

He pulled the car away from the motel and out onto the county road.

"What about granola?" I said.

"Have to go over to Atlanta for that," Becker said. "People in Columbia County don't eat granola and don't tolerate those who do."

I poured a little container of cream into a paper cup full of coffee and stirred in several sugars. I drank some, and fished out a large biscuit with a sausage patty in the middle.

"Okay," I said. "I'll make do."

"Figured you'd eat most things," Becker said.

"What about the horse shooting?"

"Stable over in Alton, Canterbury Farms, somebody snuck around their stable last night, shot a filly named Carolina Moon."

"Dead?"

"Don't know," Becker said. "Just picked it up off the wire. Got no jurisdiction, you know, over in South Carolina."

"Me either," I said.

"Hell, you got no jurisdiction anywhere," Becker said.

"It's very freeing," I said.

I drank some more coffee as the Georgia landscape gave way with no discernible change to the South Carolina landscape. I checked my arteries. Blood still seemed to be getting through, so I had another sausage biscuit.

I was experiencing a little of the separateness I always felt when I was away from Susan. It wasn't unreality exactly, it was more a sense that there was a large empty space around me. Even now, sitting in a squad car, maybe eighteen inches from another guy, there was a sense of crystalline isolation. It was not loneliness, nor did the feeling make me unhappy. It was simply a feeling different from any other, a feeling available only when I was away from Susan. I was alone.

"What do you know about the Clive family?" I said.

"Somebody been shooting their horses," Becker said.

"Besides that," I said. "Any of them had any problems with the law?"

"Clives are the most important family in the whole Columbia County," Becker said. "They don't have trouble with the law."

"Have they come to the attention of the law?" I said.

We were driving along a two-lane highway now. There were fields with farm equipment standing idle, and occasionally a Safeway market or a Burger King. Traffic was light. Becker kept his eyes on the road.

"You got a reason for asking?" he said.

"I'm practicing to be a detective," I said. "Plus the family seems to be full of people who would get in trouble."

" 'Cept for Penny."

"Except for her," I said.

"Old man's calmed down some, since Dolly came aboard."

"But before that?"

"Well. For a while he was married to the girls' mother. Don't remember her name right this minute. But she was a hippie."

"Lot of hippies around thirty years ago," I said.

"Yep, and that's when they got married. But times

changed and she didn't. 'Bout ten years ago she ran off with a guy played in a rock band."

"So Penny would have been about fifteen."

"Yep. The other girls were a little older."

"They're two years apart," I said. "So they'd have been seventeen and nineteen."

"See that," Becker said. "You been detecting more than you pretend."

"I'm a modest guy," I said. "How was the divorce?"

"Don't know nothing about the divorce."

"Was there a divorce?"

"Don't know. Not my department."

"So what was Clive doing between the hippie and Dolly?"

"Everything he could," Becker said.

There was a two-wheeled horse-drawn piece of farm machinery inching along in our lane. I didn't know anything about farm machinery, but this looked as if it had something to do with hay. A black man in overalls and a felt hat was sitting up on the rig, though he didn't seem to be paying much attention. The horse appeared to be the one on duty. Becker slowed as we approached it and swerved carefully out to pass.

"Booze, women, that sort of thing?"

"A lot of both," Becker said.

"Ah, sweet bird of youth," I said.

Becker grinned without looking at me.

"You hang around those Clive girls, you might get younger yourself," he said.

"While Clive's living the male fantasy life," I said, "who's looking after the girls?"

"Don't know," Becker said.

"Is there anything in this for me?" I said. "Clive screw somebody's wife, and somebody wants to get even? He sleep with some woman and ditch her and she wants to get even?"

"I don't pay attention to shit like that," Becker said. "Do I look like Ann Landers?"

"You look sort of like Archie Moore," I said. "And you sound like a guy who knows things he's not saying."

"It's a special talent," Becker said.

"The real talent is sounding like you don't know anything you're not telling," I said.

"I can do that," Becker said.

"If you want to," I said.

Becker watched the road.

"So why don't you want to?"

We passed a sign that read, "Welcome to Alton."

"Because you want me to wonder."

Becker slowed and turned into a narrow dirt road that went under high pines, limbless the first thirty feet or so up. I remembered it from my last visit, eight years ago.

"You want me to look into them, but you don't want it to have come from you, because it could come back and bite you in the ass."

"Clives the most powerful family in Columbia County," Becker said, and turned off the dirt road into a wide clearing and parked near a white rail fence near the Canterbury Farms training track.

FOURTEEN

WE DIDN'T LEARN much in Alton. An Alton County Sheriff's detective named Felicia Boudreau was on the case. I knew her from eight years earlier, and Becker and I talked with her sitting in her car at the stable site.

Carolina Moon, she told us, had been a filly of modest promise. Her groom had found her dead in her stall when he went to feed her in the morning. She'd been shot once in the neck with a .22 long bullet, which had punctured her aorta, and the horse had bled to death.

"We have the bullet," Felicia said. "Vet took it out of the horse."

"We'd like to see if we can match it against ours," Becker said.

Felicia said, "Sure."

"Nothing else?" I said.

"Well, it's nice to see you again," she said.

"You too," I said. "Got any clues?"

"None."

"Lot of that going around," I said.

"What's it been, eight years?"

"Yep. Still getting your hair done in Batesburg?" I said.

"Yes, I am."

"Still looks great," I said.

"Yes, it does."

We talked with Frank Ferguson, who owned the horse. He didn't have any idea why someone would shoot his horse. I remembered him from the last time I was in Alton, but he didn't remember me. He had been smoking a meerschaum pipe when I talked with him eight years before. I thought of saying something about it, but decided it would be showing off, especially after my hair-done-in-Batesburg triumph.

We headed back toward Lamarr in the late afternoon with neither information nor lunch. I didn't mind about the lunch. The sausage biscuits from breakfast were still sticking to my ribs. In fact, I was considering the possibility that I might never have to eat again.

"That didn't help much," Becker said.

"No," I said, "just widened the focus a little."

We were heading west now and the afternoon sun was coming straight in at us. Becker put down his sun visor.

"Maybe it was supposed to," Becker said.

"So we wouldn't concentrate entirely on the Clives?" I said.

Becker shrugged.

"What is this, you give me an answer and I try to think up the question?"

Becker grinned, squinting into the sun.

"Like that game show," he said. "On TV."

"Swell," I said.

We kept driving straight into the sun. The landscape along the highway was red clay and pines and fields in which nothing much seemed to be growing.

"Okay, let me just expostulate for a while," I said. "You can nod or not as you wish."

"Expostulate?" Becker said.

"I'm sleeping with a Harvard grad," I said.

"The Emory of the North," Becker said.

"I have a series of crimes which, excepting only Carolina Moon," I said, "centers on a family made up of Pud, who's an alcoholic bully, and SueSue, who's an alcoholic sexpot, and Cord, who likes young boys, and Stonie, who, according to SueSue, is sexually frustrated. They are mothered by Hippie, who ran off with a guitar player while her daughters were in their teens, and Walter, who after Hippie ran off, consoled himself by bopping everything that would hold still long enough."

"And Penny," Becker said.

"Who seems to run the business."

"Pretty well too," Becker said.

"You know anything about any of these things?" I said.

"Heard Cord might be a chicken wrangler," Becker said.

"How about Stonie?"

Becker shrugged.

"SueSue?"

Shrug.

"How about good old Pud?" I said.

"Pud's pretty much drunk from noon on, every day," Becker said.

"Probably doesn't make for a good marriage."

"I ain't a social worker," Becker said. "I don't keep track of everybody's dick."

"Still, you knew about Cord."

"I am a police officer," he said.

"Okay, so Cord got in trouble."

Becker didn't comment. We pulled into the parking lot of my motel. Becker stopped by the front door. We sat for a moment in silence.

"These are important people, probably the most important people in Columbia County," Becker said. "Walter Clive is a personal friend of the sheriff of Columbia County, who I work for."

"You mentioned that," I said.

"So I don't want you going down to the Bath House Bar and Grill and nosing around there, asking questions about Cord Wyatt."

"I can see why you wouldn't," I said. "That the gay scene in Lamarr?"

"Such as it is," Becker said. "Tedy Sapp, bouncer down there, used to be a deputy of mine, spells it with one *d* in Tedy, and two *p*'s in Sapp. When you don't go down there like I told you not to, I don't want you talking to him or mentioning my name."

"Sure," I said. "Stay away from the Bath House Bar and Grill, and don't talk to Sapp the bouncer. Where is it located so I can be sure not to go near it?"

"Mechanic Street."

"I'll be careful," I said.

We sat for a while longer in silence.

"The family is peculiar," I said.

"And the horse shooting is peculiar," Becker said.

"What does this suggest?" I said.

"Can't imagine," Becker said.

FIFTEEN

THE BATH HOUSE Bar and Grill had a Bud Light sign in its front window with a neon tube image of Spuds McKenzie looking raffish and thirsty. The room was air-conditioned. There was a bar the length of the room across the back. There were tables in front of the bar. Along the right wall there was a small dance floor, with a raised platform for live performances. At the moment the music, Bette Midler singing something I didn't recognize, was from a big old-fashioned Wurlitzer jukebox next to the door. Behind the bar was a chalkboard with the night's by-the-glass wine selections, and a list of bar food specials. In the late afternoon, the bar was about half occupied and there were people at several of the tables. It was like any other place where people went to avoid being alone, except that all the customers were men.

The bartender had a crew cut and a mustache and a

tan. He was wearing a dark green polo shirt and chino pants. I ordered a draft beer.

"Tedy around?" I said.

"Tedy?"

"Tedy Sapp," I said.

"Table over there." The bartender nodded. "With the muscles."

Tedy was wearing the Bath House uniform—green polo shirt, chino pants, and a tan. His hair was colored the aggressively artificial blond color that musicians and ballplayers were affecting that year. It was cut very short. He was a flagrant bodybuilder. About my size, and probably about my weight. He was chiseled and cut and buffed like a piece of statuary. I picked up my beer.

"That'll be three and a quarter," the bartender said.

I put a five on the bar and carried my beer over to Tedy's table. He looked up, moving his eyes without moving his head. He had the easy manner of someone who was confident that he could knock you on your ass. He had a cup of coffee in front of him on the table, and a copy of the *Atlanta Constitution* was folded next to it.

"My name's Spenser," I said. "Dalton Becker mentioned you to me."

"Becker's a good guy," Sapp said.

His voice carried a whisper of hoarseness. He gestured at an empty chair, and I sat down.

"You used to work for Becker," I said.

"Used to work for Becker," he said. "Deputy sheriff. 'Fore that I was in the Army—airborne. Lifted weights. Karate. Married. Trying as hard as I could to be straight."

"And you weren't," I said.

"Nope. Wasn't, am not now. Doesn't look like I'm gonna be."

"And now you're not trying," I said.

"Nope. Got divorced, quit the cops."

"Becker fire you when you came out?"

"Nope. I coulda stayed on. I wanted to quit."

"Still pumping a little iron, though," I said.

"That works gay or straight," Sapp said.

"And now you're here?"

"Yep. Four to midnight six days a week."

"Hard work?" I said.

"No. Now and then a couple queens get into a hissy-fit fight, scratching and kicking, and I have to settle them down. But mostly I'm here so that a few good old boys won't get drunk and come in here to bash some fairies."

"That happen very often?" I said.

"Not as often as it used to," Sapp said.

"Because you're here."

"Yep."

"Most people don't anticipate a tough fairy," I said.

Sapp grinned. "You look like you might have swapped a couple punches in your life."

"You ever lose?" I said.

"What? A fight? In here? Naw."

"That why you quit the cops?" I said. "So you could work here?"

"Yep."

"So you could protect the people who come here?"

Sapp shrugged.

"Lot of gay guys never really learned how to fight," he said.

"Most straight guys too," I said.

Sapp nodded.

"Well, I know how," Sapp said. "And I figured I could maybe serve and protect . . ." He stopped and thought about how he wanted to say it. "With a little more focus, down here, than I could working out of the Columbia County Sheriff's substation."

I sipped some of my beer. He drank some coffee.

"What do you do?" Sapp said. "I know you're carrying a piece."

"Alert," I said. "Detective. Private. From Boston."

"I figured you wasn't from down heah in the old Confederacy," Sapp said.

"Lawzy me, no," I said.

My instinct told me I could level with Sapp. My instinct has been wrong before, but I decided to trust it this time.

"I'm down here working for Walter Clive," I said, "trying to find out who's been shooting his horses."

"Horses?"

"Yep, apparently at random, several of them. He's worried now about a two-year-old named Hugger Mugger, who's supposed to be on his way to the Triple Crown."

"And after that a lifetime of stud fees," Sapp said.

Without being asked, the bartender came over with coffee for Sapp and a beer for me. He put them down, picked up the empties, and went away.

"So why come talking to me?" Sapp said.

"You know the Clive family?"

"Un-huh. Everybody in Columbia County knows the Clives."

"I'm interested in the son-in-law, Cord Wyatt."

Sapp didn't say anything. He put sugar in his coffee, added some cream, and stirred slowly.

"I am told he is interested in young boys," I said.

Sapp stirred his coffee some more. I suspected he was consulting with his instincts.

"So what if he was?" Sapp said.

"I'm told he acts out that interest."

"And?"

"I think adults have no business scoring children, but that's not the point."

"What is the point?"

"The family is strange," I said. "The crime is strange. Does that mean the crime comes from the family? I don't know. I'm trying to find out."

Sapp drank some more coffee. He nodded.

"I see how you're thinking," he said. "I was a cop once."

"Me too," I said.

"Why'd you quit?"

"I got fired. Disobedience."

"I'll bet you're pretty good at disobedience," Sapp said.

"One of my best things," I said.

I drank some more beer. Sapp drank some more coffee. The jukebox played a song I'd never heard before, sung by a woman I didn't know. The lyrics had something to do with a barroom in Texas. Two guys got up and slow-danced to it on the dance floor.

"I know Wyatt," Sapp said.

"He come in here?"

"Not very much," Sapp said. "I do some counseling too, on, ah, gender identity issues."

"Wyatt came to you?"

"Yeah."

"What can you tell me?"

"Anything I want. I'm not licensed or anything. I know something about gender identity issues. I just talk to people."

"What do you want to tell me about Wyatt?" I said.

"He's fighting it," Sapp said. "Something I know a little about. He wants to be straight and rich and have nice teeth."

"Man's reach must exceed his grasp. . . ." I said.

"So he sits on the feelings and sits on them and finally he can't sit on them anymore and he goes off the wagon, so to speak."

"Kids?" I said.

Sapp nodded.

"Prostitutes mostly," Sapp said. "In Augusta."

"He ever get in trouble about it?"

"Yeah. Augusta Vice got him in a street sweep once, Clive got him off. He moved on a kid here in Lamarr once. Kid's mother called the cops."

"Clive get it buried?" I said.

"Yep."

"Money?"

"And fear. Delroy does it for him."

"I don't see Becker taking a bribe."

"Nope, but his boss will."

"Delroy the bagman?"

"Yep."

"What about the fear?"

"Delroy offers money to the kid's family. They don't take it, he tells them that something bad will happen to the kid."

"Wyatt tell you this?" I said.

"No."

"You talked with the kid," I said.

"Couple years afterwards," he said.

"He came to you?"

"Yeah," Sapp said. "He was afraid he was gay. I told him I thought he'd been exploited by Wyatt. I told him if anyone threatened him again he was to come right straight to me and we'd see about it."

"Anyone threaten him again?"

"No."

"Is he gay?" I said.

"I don't think so," Sapp said.

"You tell him that?"

"I'm not looking for converts," Sapp said. "I told him it's not important to be straight or gay. It's important to be what you are."

"Like you," I said.

Sapp grinned at me.

"I'm queer, and I'm here," he said.

"Know anything else about the Clive family that would interest me?" I said.

"Not much. I got a friend might be able to help you out, though. She's done some business with the other son-in-law. Whatsisname, Pud."

"How's she know Pud?" I said.

"She's a madame."

"In Lamarr?"

"In Lamarr."

"And how does she know you?"

"She's a member of the gay community," Sapp said.

SIXTEEN

THE HOUSE SAT on a nice lawn behind a white fence, on a wide tree-lined street where other houses sat on nice lawns behind white fences. All the houses dated from before the Civil War and, had they been a little grander, would have thus qualified as antebellum mansions. I parked in the driveway and walked up to the front door and rang the bell. The yard smelled richly of flowers. In a minute the door was opened by a smallish woman in jeans and a white shirt. She wore no shoes. Her toenails were painted dark maroon. Her gray-blond hair was twisted into a single long braid that reached nearly to her waist.

I said, "Polly Brown?"

"Yes."

"My name is Spenser. Tedy Sapp sent me over."

"Tedy called me," she said.

She stepped out onto the porch and closed the door behind her.

"We can sit on the veranda," she said. "It's such a pleasant night."

We sat in a couple of rocking chairs and looked out across the dark lawn at the quiet street. There was a good breeze blowing past us and it must have discouraged the bugs, because there weren't any.

"This is not a whorehouse," Polly Brown said. "I run an escort service. My girls come to you."

"I'm not here for that," I said.

"I know why you're here, I was just clarifying my situation. The 'you' was generalized."

"Of course it was," I said. "You don't sound southern."

"I'm from Cincinnati," she said. "Went to college and everything."

"How'd you end up here?"

"I have no idea," she said.

We were quiet again, rocking in the near darkness.

"So what would you like to know about Pud Potter?" she said.

"I gather he availed himself of your services."

"Often," she said.

"But not here."

"I told you."

"Yes, you did, so where?"

"Where would I send the girl?"

"Yes. I assume it wasn't to his house."

"Oh, wouldn't that be smart," she said. " 'Hello, Mrs. Potter, I'm here to fuck your husband.' "

"So where?" I said.

"He keeps a room and bath in town. Just off the square."

"Glad to hear there's a bath," I said.

"So what's the problem?" Polly said.

"My question exactly," I said. "He ever cause trouble or anything?"

"Pud? Hell no, he's a sweetheart. Lotta the girls liked him because he'd be too drunk to actually do anything and they'd get paid anyways."

"How about the law?" I said. "He ever have any trouble there?"

"Nope. I run a clean operation, pay my dues, the law leaves me alone."

"Including Becker?"

"The black deputy-in-charge?"

"Un-huh."

"I have no problem with him."

"You pay him off?"

"No."

"Operation like this pays off somebody," I said.

She rocked a little and didn't say anything. She was small enough so that her feet only touched the floor when she rocked forward.

"But not Becker," she said.

"Know a guy named Delroy?"

"Maybe. What's he do?"

"Private security," I said. "On behalf of Pud's father-in-law."

"Yes. I know him."

A silver Volvo station wagon went slowly past us on

the empty street, its headlights bright and silent.

"Tell me about him?"

"One of the girls tried to supplement her income," Polly said, "by putting the squeeze on Pud."

"Threaten to tell his wife?"

"Worse. She rigged a Polaroid and got some pictures during the gig."

"Which she threatened to show his wife."

"And everybody else, I believe."

"And?"

"And Delroy came down and explained the facts of life to her."

"Which were?"

"I never asked."

"Can I talk with her?"

Polly shrugged.

"If you can find her," she said. "Name's Jane Munroe."

"You know where I should look?"

"No."

"She doesn't work for you anymore?"

"No. I fired her before Delroy even talked to her."

"He talk to you first?"

"Yes. He suggested I fire her, but I would have anyway. Nothing kills a good client list like some whore threatening to blab."

"Is Jane still in town?"

"I'm not their mother," Polly said. "I manage their professional lives. I have no idea where Jane Munroe is, or if she's still using the name."

"Was Delroy polite?"

"Very businesslike," she said.

"He threaten you?"

"Didn't need to. As soon as I heard about the scam, I told him she'd be fired."

A big yellow cat appeared and rubbed up against my leg. I reached down and scratched his ear. He stayed for a moment, then left me and jumped up onto the porch railing and sat looking out over the dark lawn.

"There anything else?"

"Like what?"

"Like something about the Clive family that I'd like to know, but am too dumb to ask?"

"Tedy said I could trust you," she said.

"Tedy's right," I said.

"How do you know Tedy? You gay?"

"I'm straight. I met him this afternoon, the way I've met you tonight."

"I haven't had a lot of reason to trust straight men," she said.

"You used to turn tricks?" I said.

"Sure. You think I bought a franchise?"

"Just being polite," I said.

"A bunch of fat guys with hair on their back," she said. "Usually drunk, telling me they loved me. Telling me that they were going to give me the fuck of my life."

She laughed. It was a very unpleasant sound in the soft Georgia night. The yellow cat turned his head and looked at her without emotion.

I waited.

"What a hoot!" she said.

"You're a lesbian," I said.

"How'd you know?"

"I'm a professional detective," I said.

"Sapp told you."

"Yes, but I questioned him closely."

"Lot of the girls are lesbians," she said.

"What's love got to do with it," I said.

"Exactly," she said.

The yellow cat turned his head back toward the dark lawn, then silently disappeared off the railing. There was a scurrying in the bushes and a small squeak and then silence. I waited some more.

"Sapp's a good man," Polly said.

"Seems so to me," I said.

"You was smarter," Polly said, "maybe you'd ask me about Stonie Clive."

"Cord Wyatt's wife?"

"Yes."

"Tell me about her," I said.

"She worked for me for a while."

"When?"

"Two years ago."

"You know who she was?"

"Not at the time."

"How'd you recruit her?"

"She came to me. Said she'd heard about me. She said she had always wanted to do this kind of work and could I take her on? She was a nice-looking girl. Upper-class. I figured she'd do well."

"So she actually worked."

"Yes. But here's the cool part. I service a truck stop on the Interstate, up by Crawfordville. Normally I send the worst girls up there. Mostly it's head in the cab of some ten-wheeler at twenty bucks a throw. Stonie wanted that."

"BJ's at a truck stop?" I said.

"If you don't waste a lot of time talking," Polly said, "you can make a pretty good night's pay."

"Why would she need money?" I said.

A little light spilled out onto the veranda through the screen door. It was enough so that I could see her shrug.

"She's not still with you?" I said.

"No. Left about six, eight months ago."

"With no notice?"

Polly almost smiled.

"Nope, just stopped showing up. Lot of girls do that."

"How'd you find out who she was?"

"Saw her picture in the paper, some big racetrack thing."

"You're sure it was Stonie?"

"I know my girls," Polly said.

"She ever say why she wanted to do this?"

"Nope."

"You have any theories?" I said.

She rocked some more.

"Most of the girls it's simple. They got no education. They got no skills. They need money. So they do this. Some girls do it because they get something out of exploiting men."

"The men are often thought to be exploiting them," I said.

"Uh-huh."

I could tell that Polly had her own position on exploitation.

"Some girls just like it," she said.

"Truck stops at twenty bucks a . . . pop?"

"Not usually. But everybody's different."

"You think Stonie liked it?"

"No."

"It wasn't the money," I said.

"I don't think it was the money," Polly said.

"Exploit men?"

"Maybe a little of that," Polly said. "But . . ."

She rocked for a time, thinking about it.

"You know her husband's a chicken fucker?"

"I know," I said.

"I think she was getting even," Polly said.

SEVENTEEN

"So what do you think?" I said.

I was lying in my shorts on the bed in the Holiday Inn in Lamarr, Georgia, talking on the phone to Susan in Cambridge, Massachusetts. She said she was in bed. Which meant that she had her hair up, and some sort of expensive glop on her face. The TV would be on, though she would have muted it when the phone rang. Almost certainly, Pearl was asleep beside her on the bed.

"I think you're trapped inside the first draft of a Tennessee Williams play."

"Without you," I said.

"I know."

"You're in bed?" I said.

"Yes."

"Naked?"

"Not exactly."

"White socks, gray sweatpants, a white T-shirt with a picture of Einstein on it?"

"You remember," she said.

"Naked makes for better phone sex," I said.

"Pretense is a slippery slope," she said.

Her voice was quite light, and not very strong, but when she was amused there were hints of a contralto substructure that enriched everything she said.

"Don't you shrinks ever take a break?" I said.

"So many fruitcakes," Susan said, "so little time."

"How true," I said. "What do you think of Polly Brown's theory that Stonie goes to truck stops to avenge herself on her husband?"

"It would be better if I had a chance to talk with her," Susan said.

"I'll be your eyes and ears," I said.

"Have you talked with her?"

"Once, at a cocktail party, for maybe a minute."

"Oh, that'll be fine then," Susan said. "No therapist could ask for more."

"Gimme a guess," I said.

"Her husband is actively gay, with a special interest in young men," Susan said.

"Yes."

"Would you say that she would experience that as him having sex in the most inappropriate way possible?"

"Yes."

"And is that what she's doing?"

"Seems so. So it is revenge?"

"Could be. Tit for tat. People often are very crude in their pathologies."

"Like me," I said. "I keep pretending you're naked on the bed."

"On the other hand, it may be more subtle than that. She may be simply enacting her condition."

"Her condition is smoking the cannoli in a parking lot?"

"It's good to know that you haven't lost that keen edge of your sophistication. Perhaps her activities in the parking lot are, at least symbolically, how she experiences herself."

"Because of her husband?"

"Not only her husband," Susan said. "You said her father got her husband out of a couple of boy-love jams."

"Yes."

"Why?"

"Appearances," I said. "Save the family from scandal."

"So he knows her marriage is probably a sham. Other than covering up for the husband, does he do anything about it?"

"Not that I can see."

"So as far as we can tell, her father and husband don't value her beyond whatever ornamental use they put her to."

"I get it," I said.

"I knew you would," Susan said.

"There's another thing bothering me," I said. "The shooting of the horse over in Alton."

"Why does that bother you?"

"Becker and I speculate that it might be to distract me," I said. "And that's a reasonable speculation."

"But?"

"But if it's the work of some kind of serial psychopath, which is what it seems like, then distracting me would seem to be too rational an act."

"Possibly," Susan said.

"I mean, the compulsion isn't about me."

"You may have been added to what it is about," Susan said.

"Or maybe it's not a compulsion," I said.

"Are you just casting about, or have you any other reason to think it's something else?"

"Well, what kind of compulsion is this? A compulsion to shoot horses, with no concern for the result?"

"No way to know," Susan said. "Compulsions are consistent only to their own logic."

"Well, I remain skeptical."

"As well you should."

"Thank you, Doctor."

"Will that be Visa or MasterCard?" Susan said.

"I'll recompense you in full," I said, "when I get home."

"Soon?"

"I have no idea."

"It's annoying, isn't it," Susan said, "to have our life scheduled by the pathology of someone we can't even identify."

"You should know," I said.

"Yes," she said. "Sometimes I think we're doing the same work."

"Do you think that absence makes the heart grow fonder?"

"No. I'm already as fond as I'm capable of being," Susan said. "Makes me miss you, though."

"Yes," I said. "I feel the same way."

"Good," Susan said. "And stay away from the truck stops."

EIGHTEEN

‑ ‑ ‑ ‑ ‑ ‑ ‑ ‑ ‑ ‑ ‑ ‑ ‑ ‑ ‑ ‑ ‑ ‑ ‑

THE HORSE SHOOTER upped the ante on a rainy Sunday night by shooting Walter Clive dead in the exercise area of Three Fillies Stables. I was there at daylight, with Becker and a bunch of Columbia County crime scene deputies.

"Exercise rider found him this morning when she came into work," Becker said. "Right there where you see him."

Where I saw him was facedown in the middle of the open paddock in front of the stables, under a tree, with the rain soaking the crime scene. Someone had rigged a polyethylene canopy over the body and the immediate crime scene, in hopes of preserving any evidence that was left.

"Where is she now?"

"In the stable office," Becker said. "I got one woman deputy, and she's in there with her."

"Will I be able to talk to her?"

"Sure."

I stepped to the body and squatted down beside it. Clive was in a white shirt and gray linen slacks. There were loafers on his feet, without socks. His silver hair was soaked and plastered to his skull. There was no sign of a wound.

"In the forehead, just above the right eyebrow," Becker said. "Photo guys are already done—you want to see?"

"Yes."

Becker had on thin plastic crime scene gloves. He reached down and turned Clive's head. There was a small black hole above his eyebrow, the flesh around it a little puffy and discolored from the entry of the slug.

"No exit wound," I said.

"That's right."

"Small caliber," I said.

"Looks like a .22 to me."

"Yes."

"Figure he caught the horse shooter in the act?" Becker said.

"Be the logical conclusion," I said.

"Yep. It would."

"Where was Security South during all this?" I said. "Busy polishing their belt buckles?"

"Security guy was in with the horse," Becker said.

"Hugger Mugger."

"Yeah. When I say the horse, that's who I mean. He heard the shot, and came out, ah, carefully, and looked around and didn't see anything, and went back inside with the horse."

"It was raining," I said.

"All night."

"How far out you figure he came?"

"His uni was dry when I talked to him," Becker said.

"No wrinkles?"

"Nope."

"Probably didn't want to be lured away from the horse."

"Hugger Mugger," Becker said.

I looked at him. He was expressionless.

"Of course Hugger Mugger," I said. "What other horse are we talking about?"

Becker grinned.

"So nobody sees anything. Nobody but the guard hears anything," Becker said. "We're looking for footprints, but it's been raining hard since yesterday afternoon."

"Crime scene isn't going to give you much," I said.

"You Yankees are so pessimistic."

"Puritan heritage," I said. "The family's been told?"

"Yep. Told them myself."

"How were they?"

"Usual shock and dismay," Becker said.

"Anything unusual?"

Becker shook his head.

"You been a cop," he said. "You've had to tell people that somebody's been murdered, what would be unusual?"

"You're right," I said. "I've seen every reaction there is. Delroy been around?"

"Not yet," Becker said.

We were quiet for a while, standing in the rain, partly sheltered by the tree, looking at how dead Walter Clive was.

"Why'd you call me?" I said.

"Two heads are better than one," Becker said.

"Depends on the heads," I said.

"In this case yours and mine," Becker said. "You been a big-city cop, you might know something."

I nodded.

"Between us," Becker said, "we might figure something out."

I nodded some more. The rain kept coming. Walter Clive kept lying there. Behind us a van with *Columbia County Medical Examiner* lettered on the side pulled up and two guys in raincoats got out and opened up the back.

"Here's what I think," I said. "I think that you are smelling a big rat here, and the rat is somewhere in the Clive family, and they are too important and too connected for a deputy sheriff to take on directly."

"They're awful important," Becker said.

"So you're using me as a surrogate. Let me take them on. You feed me just enough to keep me looking, but not enough to get you in trouble. If I come up with something, you can take credit for it after I've gone back to Boston. If I get my ass handed to me, you can shake your head sadly and remark what a shame it was that I'm nosy."

"Man do that would be a devious man," Becker said.

"Sho' 'nuff," I said.

NINETEEN

$\text{-- -- -- -- -- -- -- -- -- -- -- -- -- -- -- -- --}$

IT WAS STILL raining when they buried Walter
Clive's cremated ashes. It had rained all week. After the
funeral, people straggled into the Clives' house and
stood under a canopy in the backyard looking glum and
uncomfortable as they ordered drinks. I was there, having nowhere else to be, and I watched as people began
to get drunk and talk about how Walter would have
wanted everyone to have a good time at his funeral.
People began to look less glum. Just the way old Walt
would have wanted it. Penny was running things. She
was sad and contained and doing fine. Jon Delroy was
there in a dark suit. The family lawyer was there, a guy
named Vallone, who looked like Colonel Sanders. Pud
and SueSue, still sober, stood with Stonie and Cord.
They were dressed just right for a funeral. Everyone was
dressed just right for a funeral, except one woman who
wore an ankle-length cotton dress with yellow flowers
on it. Her hair was gray-blond and hung straight to her

waist. She wore huge sunglasses and sandals. Penny brought her over.

"This is my mother," she said, "Sherry Lark."

"It was nice of you to come," I said, to be saying something.

"Oh, it's not Walter. It's my girls. In crisis girls need their mother."

I could see Penny wrinkle her nose. I nodded.

"Yes," I said.

"Walter was lost to me an eternity past, but the girls are part of my soul."

"Of course," I said. "Have you remarried?"

"No. I don't think marriage is a natural thing for people."

She was drinking what looked like bourbon on the rocks. Which was probably a natural thing for people.

"So is Lark your, ah, birth name?"

"No. It's my chosen name. When I left Walter I didn't want to keep his name. And I didn't want to return to my father's name, about which I had no choice when I was born."

"I had the same problem," I said. "They just stuck me with my father's name."

She paid no attention to me. She was obviously comfortable talking about herself.

"So I took a name that symbolizes the life I was seeking, the soaring airborne freedom of a lark."

She drank some bourbon. I nodded and smiled.

"I relate to that," I said. "I'm thinking of changing my name to Eighty-second Airborne."

She didn't respond. She was one of those people that,

if you say something they don't understand, they pretend you haven't spoken.

"Come along, Mother," Penny said. "You really must say hello to Senator Thompson."

Penny gave me a look over her shoulder as she moved her mother away. I smiled neutrally. I had a beer because I was sure that's how old Walt would have wanted it. I took a small swallow. A black woman in a little maid's suit passed a tray of stuffed mushrooms. I declined. Smoked salmon with endive and a dab of crème fraîche came by. I declined it too. The governor of Georgia came in. He went straight to Dolly, the bereaved mistress, and took her hand in both of his. They spoke briefly. He kissed her cheek. She gestured toward her son, and Jason and the governor shook hands. Dolly's face was pale beneath her perfect makeup, and the attractive smile lines around her mouth were deeper than I remembered.

The rain drummed steadily on the canvas canopy roof, and dripped off the edges in a steady drizzle. Dutch, the family Dalmatian, made his way through the crowd, alert for stuffed mushrooms, and found me and remembered me and wagged his tail. I snagged a little crab cake from the passing tray and handed it to Dutch. He took it from me, gently, and swallowed it whole. I watched Stonie and Cord. They stood together, looking very good, and taking condolences gravely. But when they weren't talking to someone, they didn't talk to each other. It was as if they had been accidentally placed together in a receiving line, one not knowing the other. Pud and SueSue were also receiving condolences. But they were less grave. In fact they were now drunk. Pud's face was very red. He was sweating. He and SueSue appeared to be arguing between condolences, although SueSue's laughter erupted regularly while she was being condoled. There was a smell of honeysuckle under the canopy and a faint smell of food coming from the kitchen as the hors d'oeuvres were prepared. Dutch sat patiently in front of me and waited for another hors d'oeuvre. I gave him a rye crisp with beef tenderloin on it, and horseradish. He took that in as quickly as he had the crab cake, though he snorted a little at the horseradish.

"You'd eat a dead crow in the street," I said to him. "And you're snorting at horseradish."

He pricked his ears a little at me, and waited. Penny came back alone. She was carrying a glass of white wine, though as far as I could tell, she hadn't drunk any.

"I apologize for my mother."

"No need," I said.

Penny laughed.

"The last hippie," she said.

"How are she and Dolly together?" I said.

"We try to see that they're not together," Penny said.

"Was Dolly in your father's life when Sherry was around?"

"I think so," she said. "Why do you ask?"

"Occupational habit," I said.

"I think it's not appropriate right now," Penny said.

"Of course it isn't."

"Could you come see me tomorrow, stable office, around ten?"

"Sure," I said.

Penny smiled to let me know that she wasn't mad, and moved over to a foursome who stood in the doorway looking for the bar. The women were wearing big hats. She kissed all of them and walked with them to the bar. Lightning rippled across the sky over the Clive house and in a few moments thunder followed. A small wind began to stir, and it seemed colder. More lightning. The thunder followed more closely now. Some dogs are afraid of thunder. Dutch wasn't. He was far too single-minded. He nudged my hand. There were no hors d'oeuvres being passed. I took a few peanuts off the bar and fed him. I looked at the crowd, now drunk and happy. It would have been the perfect moment to call for silence and announce that I had solved the case. Except that I hadn't solved the case. So far since I'd been here I hadn't caught the horse shooter, and the guy who hired me had been murdered. I didn't have a clue who was shooting the horses, and I had absolutely no idea who had shot Walter Clive.

Spenser, ace detective.

TWENTY

"I LIKE YOU," Penny said. "And I think you're a smart man."

"I haven't proved it so far," I said.

"You've done your best. How can you figure out the mind of a madman."

"You think all this is the work of a madman?"

"Of course, don't you?"

"Just that occupational knee jerk," I said. "Somebody says something, I ask a question."

"I understand," she said.

We were sitting in the stable office. It was still drizzling outside. The crime scene tape was gone. There was no sign that Walter Clive had died there. The horses were all in their stalls, looking out now and then, but discouraged by the sporadic rain.

"With Daddy's death," Penny said, "I have the responsibility of running things, and I don't know how it's going to go. Daddy ran so much of this business out of his hip pocket. Handshakes, personal phone calls, promises made over martinis. I don't know how long it will take me to get control of it all and see where I am."

"And you have your sisters to support," I said.

"Their husbands do that," Penny said.

"And who supports the husbands?"

She dipped her head in acknowledgment.

"I guess they didn't just get their jobs through the help-wanted ads, did they," she said.

"And I'll bet they couldn't get comparable pay somewhere else," I said.

"That's unkind," Penny said.

"But true," I said.

She smiled.

"But true."

I waited.

"Look at me sitting at Daddy's desk, in Daddy's office. I feel like a little girl that's snuck in where I shouldn't be."

"You're where you should be," I said.

"Thank you."

We sat.

"This is hard," Penny said.

I didn't know what "this" was. Penny paused and took in a long breath.

"I'm going to have to let you go," she said.

I nodded.

"I don't want any but the most necessary expenses. The investigation is in the hands of the police now, and with my father's death, they are fully engaged."

"I saw the governor at the wake," I said.

"When it was just some horses, and not terribly valuable ones at that," Penny said, "no one was working that hard on it. Now that Daddy's been killed . . ."

"It has their attention," I said. "I can stick around *pro bono* for a while."

"I couldn't ask you to do that."

"It's not just for you," I said. "I don't like having a client shot out from under me."

"I know, but no. I thank you for what you've done, and for being so decent a man. But I'd prefer that you left this to the police."

"Okay," I said.

"Please send me your final bill," she said.

"Against the private eye rules," I said. "Your client gets shot, you don't bill his estate."

"It's not your fault," she said. "I want a final bill."

"Sure," I said.

"You're not going to send one, are you."

"No."

I stood. She stood.

"You're a lovely man," she said. "Would you like to say goodbye to Hugger?"

I had no feelings one way or another about Hugger, but horse people are like that and she'd just called me a lovely man.

"Sure," I said.

"Give him a carrot," she said, and handed me one.

We walked in the now more insistent rain along the stable row until we came to Hugger's stall. He looked out, keeping his head stall side of the drip line, his big dark eyes looking, I suspected, far more profound than he was. I handed him a carrot on my open palm, and he lipped it in. I patted his nose and turned and Penny stood on her tiptoes and put her arms around my neck and gave me a kiss on the lips.

"Take care of yourself," she said.

"You too," I said.

The kiss was sisterly, with no heat in it, but she stayed leaning against me, with her arms still around my neck, and her head thrown back so she could look up at me.

"I'm sorry things didn't work out," she said.

"Me too," I said.

We stayed that way for a minute. Then she let go of me and stepped back and looked at me for another moment and turned and walked back to the stable office. I watched her go, and then turned the collar of my jacket up to keep the rain off my neck and headed for my car.

TWENTY-ONE

I ARRIVED BACK in Boston around three-thirty. By quarter to five I was in Susan's living room, showered and shaved and aromatic with aftershave, waiting for her when she got through work. I was sitting on the couch with Pearl, having a drink, when Susan came upstairs from her last patient.

She saw me, and smiled, and said hello, and patted Pearl and gave her a kiss, and walked past us into her bedroom. I could hear the shower, and in about fifteen minutes, Susan reappeared wearing a bath towel. She flipped the towel open and shut, like a flasher.

"Y'all want to get on in heah, Georgia boy?"

"That's the worst southern accent I've ever heard," I said.

"I know," she said, "but everything else will be pretty good."

"How could you be so sure I'd be responsive?" I said. "Maybe I'm tired from the long drive."

"I'm a psychotherapist," Susan said. "I know these things."

"Amazing."

When we made love, Susan liked to do the same things every time, which was less boring than it sounds, because it included about everything either of us knew how to do. She was also quite intense about it. Sometimes she was so fully in the moment that she seemed to have gone to a place I'd never been. Sometimes it took her several minutes, when we were through, to resurface.

As usual, when she had come back sufficiently, she got up and opened the bedroom door. Pearl came in and jumped on the bed and snuffled around, as if she suspected what might have happened here, and disapproved.

There was the usual jockeying for position before we finally got Pearl out from between us. She settled, as she always did, with a noise that suggested resignation, near the foot of the bed, and curled up and lay still, only her eyes moving as she watched Susan and me reintegrate our snuggle.

"Postcoital languor is more difficult with Pearl," Susan said.

"But not impossible," I said.

"Nothing's impossible for us."

I looked at the familiar form of the crown molding along the edge of Susan's bedroom ceiling. On the dresser was a big color photograph of Susan and me, taken fifteen years ago on a balcony in Paris, not long after she had come back from wherever the hell she had been. We looked pretty happy.

"We were pretty happy in that picture," I said.

"We had reason to be."

"Yes."

"We still do."

"Yes."

"Would you be happier now if Mr. Clive hadn't been killed in Georgia?"

"Yes."

"Even though you were not responsible for him getting killed, nor could you have been expected to prevent it?"

"Yes."

"Send not therefore asking for whom the bell tolls," Susan said.

"Well, sometimes," I said, "it actually does toll for thee."

"I know."

"On the other hand," I said, "we do what we can, not what we ought to."

"I know."

"And you can't win 'em all," I said.

"True."

"And all that glitters is not gold," I said.

"And a bird in the hand is worth two in the bush," Susan said.

"I always thought that saying was sort of backwards," I said.

I couldn't see her face: it was too close to my neck. But I could feel her smile.

"Well-bred Jewesses from Swampscott, Massachusetts," she said, "do not lie naked in bed and talk about bushes."

"Where did you go wrong?" I said.

"I don't know, but isn't it good that I did?"

At the foot of the bed, Pearl lapped one of her forepaws noisily. Susan rubbed my chest lightly with her right hand.

"Is there anything you can do to clean that up in Georgia?" she said.

"No one wants me to," I said.

"When has that ever made a difference to you?" Susan said.

"I have no client," I said. "No standing in the case."

"You think it was the person shooting the horses?"

"Reasonable guess," I said. "I had no clue who was doing that, and no clue really about where to go next."

"And?"

"And," I said, "I've been away from you about as long as I can stand."

"Good."

"So I'm going to put this one in the loss column and start thinking about the next game."

"Wise," Susan said.

"After all," I said, "a bush in the hand . . ."

"Never mind," Susan said.

TWENTY-TWO

‑ ‑

IT WAS MONDAY morning, bright, still early June and not very hot. I was in my office, drinking coffee and reading the paper while I waited for business. I'd drunk my allotment of coffee, and read the paper, and put it away before any showed up, but when it came it was interesting. A woman came into my office, briskly, as if offices were designed for her to walk into. I began to stand up. She indicated there was no need to, but by that time I was on my feet anyway.

"I'm Valerie Hatch," she said, and put out her hand. "You're Spenser."

"Right on both counts," I said, and shook her hand.

"Owen Brooks suggested I might speak to you about my situation. You know Owen?"

"Yes."

Owen Brooks was, improbably, the district attorney of Suffolk County. He was black, Harvard-educated, smart, humorous, pleasant, tolerant, and tougher than a Kevlar gumdrop. In a political office, he seemed primarily concerned with the successful prosecution of criminals.

"He said this was a circumstance that might best be dealt with informally, that is to say, by someone like yourself."

"Then it will have to be myself," I said. "There's no one else like me."

"Owen also told me that you found yourself amusing."

"How do you know Owen?" I said.

"I am a litigator at a major law firm in this city—which one is not germane to my reason for being here."

"Sure," I said. "What is your reason?"

"I am a single mother," she said. "And a woman with a career. To balance those two responsibilities I employ a nanny."

"That's what I'd do," I said.

She paid no attention to me. I didn't feel bad. I was pretty sure she didn't pay much attention to anyone, engrossed as she was with being a single mother and a woman with a career.

"Kate is a lovely girl," Valerie said, "but she has made some unwise choices in her past life, and one of them now threatens not only my nanny but my child."

"Kate is the nanny?" I said.

Valerie looked surprised. "Yes. Kate Malloy."

"And what is her problem?" I said.

"She is being stalked by a former lover."

"She been to the cops?" I said.

"She has, and I've spoken with Owen. We have a restraining order, but . . ." She shrugged.

I could tell that she didn't like shrugging. She wasn't used to it. She was used to nodding decisively.

"She call the cops when the lover shows up?" I said.

"Yes. Sometimes they come promptly. Sometimes they don't."

"What is the lover's name?"

"*Ex*-lover. His name is Kevin Shea."

"Has Kevin threatened her?"

"Yes. And he poses a threat to my child."

"Whose name is?"

"Miranda."

"And she's how old?"

"Sixteen months. Why are you asking all these questions?"

"So I can follow what you say. Has Kevin harmed Kate?"

"When they were together he beat her."

"And has he threatened Miranda?"

"His presence threatens Miranda. Kate can't take care of her if she's being harassed by this ape."

"And you wish to employ me?" I said.

"Yes. Owen said you were the man."

"What do you wish to employ me to do?"

"Make him go away."

"Do you have a course of action in mind?"

"No, of course not, how would I? That's what you're supposed to know. I wish he were dead."

"Dead is not generally a part of the service," I said.

She shook her head as if a fly were annoying her.

"It was just a remark. I am at my wit's end. I need you to help me straighten this out."

"Okay," I said.

"How much do you charge?"

I told her.

"Isn't that a lot of money?" she said.

"You came here asking me to save your child," I said.

"So you boosted the price?"

"No. That's the price. I was trying to help you decide if it's worth paying."

"By playing on a mother's guilt?"

I didn't remember anything about guilt, but I let it ride.

"Can you do it?"

"Sure," I said. "I can eat this guy's lunch."

"Do you require payment to start?"

"No. I'll bill you when it's done."

"What are you going to do?"

"I'll speak with Kate."

"She's very frightened. You'll have to be careful with her."

"I'll need an address."

Valerie took out a business card and wrote on the back.

"I'd prefer that you talk to her when I'm there."

"Sure."

"This evening?"

"Yes."

"Seven?"

"Fine."

She stood. I stood.

"Where is Kate now?"

"I sent her and Miranda to my mother's home in

Brookline," Valerie said. "Until I could arrange for her safety. That's the address on the back of my card."

"I'll meet you there," I said.

She looked at me the way people look at racehorses before the auction.

"Well, you look as if you'd be formidable," she said.

"You should see me in my red cape," I said.

"I'm sure I should," she said.

TWENTY-THREE

I TALKED WITH Kate in the living room of a big half-timbered Tudor-style house on a side road off of Route 9 not very far from Longwood Tennis Club. Miranda made a brief appearance in joint custody of Valerie's mother and a Shih Tzu named Buttons. Miranda seemed overdressed to me, and mildly uneasy. But I was inexpert with sixteen-month-old kids. The Shih Tzu sniffed my ankles thoughtfully, and then followed Miranda and her grandmother from the room.

"The dog is a Shih Tzu?" I said.

Valerie said it was.

"Knew a woman in Ames, Iowa, had one of those."

"How nice," Valerie said.

"Dog's name was Buttons too."

Valerie smiled stiffly.

Beside Valerie, on the yellow-flowered couch in a bay of the overdecorated living room, was a plain young

woman with red hair and very white skin. I sat on a has-
sock in front of the couch.

"You're Kate," I said.

"Yes, sir."

"And you are being stalked by a man named Kevin
Shea," I said.

"Yes, sir."

"What's your relationship to him?" I said.

"We're not related."

"Were you lovers?"

"Yes, sir."

"And now you're not."

"No, sir."

"What does he do when he stalks you?" I said.

"He follows me around."

"Does he speak to you?"

"Yes, sir."

"What does he say?"

"He swears at me and stuff."

"Does he threaten you?"

"He says if he can't have me no one else will."

"Has he ever hurt you?"

"You mean now, when he follows me?"

"At any time," I said.

"Yes, sir."

Slow going. I felt that I'd had better conversations
with Hugger Mugger.

"What did he do?" I said.

"He hit me once, when we lived together."

"Was he drunk?"

"Oh yes, sir. He drinks a lot. Says it's the only way to deal with the pain."

"What was it that attracted you to him?" I said.

"He loved me."

"And now, why is he stalking you, do you think?"

"Because he loves me. He can't bear to give me up."

Valerie said, "Kate, that's ridiculous."

"And how do you feel about him?" I said.

"I'm afraid of him. He's so crazy in love with me. I don't know what he'll do."

"How would you like me to handle this?" I said.

"I don't want him to get in trouble," Kate said.

Valerie was appalled.

"For God's sake," she said. "Kate!"

"Well, I don't," Kate said. "He loves me."

"How can you say that?" Valerie said. "He has beaten you. He threatens to kill you. This isn't love, it's obsession."

"I don't know about that psychology stuff. But I know he's crazy about me."

"He's crazy, all right," Valerie said.

Kate's small, pale face pinched up a little tighter. She wasn't going to give up the great romance of her life.

"So," I said. "If you care this much about him, why did you leave him?"

"Kevin wasn't working. There was no money. I needed this job."

I looked at Valerie Hatch.

"I told Kate that her responsibility was Miranda, and that she couldn't exercise that responsibility properly if her low-life boyfriend was hanging around."

I nodded.

"You live in?" I said to Kate.

"Yes, sir, in Ms. Hatch's place on Commonwealth Avenue."

"We have a large condominium," Valerie said. "Near the corner of Dartmouth."

"So if you live there, and Ms. Hatch doesn't want him around, you don't get to see him much."

"No, sir, hardly at all."

"When do you see him?"

"When I'm walking Miranda, or at the playground."

"Are you afraid of Kevin?" I said.

"Yes, sir, he's so angry."

"Why don't you quit this job and go back and live with Kevin?"

Valerie said, "Spenser, dammit . . ."

I put a hand up for her to be quiet. Surprisingly, she was.

"I need the money," Kate said. "And Miranda. I don't want to leave Miranda."

"You care about the kid," I said.

"I love her."

I nodded.

"I don't see where you are going with these questions," Valerie said.

"I never do either, until I ask them."

"Kevin Shea is an uneducated, unemployed drunk," Valerie said. "I don't want him around my daughter, or my daughter's nanny. And quite frankly, I don't want my daughter's nanny living with such a person."

"I think I can follow that," I said.

"I should hope so," Valerie said.

"Can you put me in touch with Kevin?" I said to Kate.

"I don't know where he's living now. He's not at the place we were."

"Is he likely to show up someplace where you are going?"

"The little park," she said. "I take Miranda there every day. He comes there a lot. And when I wheel her carriage along the river."

"You never led me to believe it was this regular," Valerie said.

"Why don't you and I go down to the park tomorrow?" I said to Kate. "And maybe walk along the river."

"I will not allow you to expose my daughter to this man," Valerie said.

"Perhaps she could stay with you," I said.

"I have a day filled with meetings tomorrow," Valerie said.

"Your mother?"

"Tomorrow is my mother's golf day."

"And I suppose Buttons isn't up to the job," I said.

"This is not a frivolous matter," Valerie said.

"See if your mother can forgo golf tomorrow," I said.

Valerie looked annoyed, but appeared ready to humor me.

"I'll meet you in front of the Commonwealth Ave. place at what, nine A.M.?" I said to Kate. "Is there a stroller or something that you normally use?"

"Yes."

"Bring it."

"Without the baby?"

"Yes."

"What if he tries to hurt me?" Kate said.

"I won't let him," I said.

"He's awfully big and strong," Kate said.

"Me too," I said.

"I don't want him to be hurt," Kate said.

"For God's sake, Kate. Listen to yourself."

Kate didn't say anything. She just stared at the rug in front of her.

"Okay," I said. "Tomorrow, you come out wheeling the stroller, and go where you usually go. Don't look for me. I'll be there, but I don't want to scare Kevin away."

"What will you do if he comes?"

"I'll reason with him," I said.

TWENTY-FOUR

THE DAY WAS somewhat overcast, and not very hot. I strolled along on the other side of the street, watching Kate Malloy as she wheeled the stroller along Commonwealth, crossed at Dartmouth, and headed for the little park. She put the stroller beside her and sat for a while on a small bench, inside the black iron fence, and watched the children and their nannies, and occasionally, maybe, their mothers. No one stalked her. No one looked like they were going to stalk her. After a while Kate got up and took the stroller and walked down Commonwealth, the rest of the way, and turned left toward the river on Arlington Street. I went along too. We crossed the pedestrian overpass to the esplanade and began to stroll west along the river. If Kevin showed up I wasn't sure what to expect. I was ready. I had a gun on my belt, and a sap in my hip pocket, and if that didn't work, I could always bite him. Still, he seemed less monstrous when Kate talked of him than he did when

Valerie talked of him. I was pretty sure I wasn't getting the whole story. I was used to it. I hadn't gotten the full story in Lamarr, Georgia. I never got the full story. There was probably something deeply philosophic going on. Maybe there was no full story. Ever.

We crossed a little footbridge over the lagoon and walked near the water. If anyone noticed that Kate was pushing an empty carriage they didn't show it. Bostonians are so reserved. There were a number of dogs being run by their owners, and a number of babies being strolled, and then there was a stalker. I didn't see him approach. He was just there all of a sudden, beside Kate, a big man wearing a tank top. His hair was in a crew cut shaved high on the sides. There were tattoos on each bicep. He took her arm. He was loud. And intense. As I closed on them I could hear him.

"I don't give a fuck about that. I need to see you. I love you."

I stopped beside them. He looked at me.

"Who the fuck are you?" he said.

He was fair-skinned and sunburned. He'd never tan darkly, but you could tell he was out-of-doors a lot.

"I'm with her," I said. "We need to talk."

"You need to take a fucking walk, pal."

He was sober, which was good news, since it was about eleven in the morning. There was no smell of booze, no slurring, none of the look around the eyes that drunks so magically achieve.

"Nope," I said. "The three of us. We'll sit down over there on that bench and we'll sort everything out."

Beside me Kate was like a rabbit, very still, quivering

with—what? Expectation? Fear? Readiness? The guy was big and strong and had probably won most of the fights he'd had. But if experience made him confident, it also gave him perspective. I could see by the way he looked at me that he wasn't sure.

"You a cop?"

"Private," I said.

He snorted. I took it as an expression of contempt.

"Sort what out?" he said. "It's that bitch she works for that needs sorting out."

"How so?" I said.

"How so? Bullshit how so," he said.

Anger got the better of perspective, and he took a swing at me. It was a pretty good swing. He didn't lead with his right. He didn't loop the punch. But he got out in front of his feet, and it made him put too much arm into the punch, and not enough body. I picked it off with my right forearm. He followed with a right that I picked off with my left forearm. It didn't deter him, so I feinted at his belly with my right. He flinched, his hands came down, and I nailed him on the jaw with a left hook that turned him half around and put him on the ground.

Kate screamed "Stop it!" and jumped in front of me and wrapped her arms around my waist and tried to push me away from Kevin. Bells were ringing for Kevin. He got halfway up and sat back down.

"He'll be all right," I said. "He's just been jarred a little. But it would be better if we left it at this. Why don't you talk with him."

She turned toward Kevin, who was sitting upright on

the ground, blinking his eyes. She dropped to her knees beside him, and put her arms around him.

"Stop it, Kevin. Please," she said. "For me. This man doesn't want to hurt you, or me. He'll help us, I know he will, if you'll talk with him. Talk with him, for me."

Kevin looked confused, but he let her help him to his feet and he walked pretty steadily with her toward the bench. When they weren't looking, I rubbed my knuckles. Every time I hit somebody my knuckles hurt. Tomorrow they'd be a little swollen, and a little sore. Occupational hazard. I couldn't go around all the time with my hands wrapped. The two of them sat on the bench. Kevin's eyes began to focus.

"Okay," I said. "We'll be friends, and I'll ask some questions, and you'll answer them and maybe we can work something out."

Neither one said anything. The hinges of Kevin's jaw were going to be very sore tomorrow.

"Don't feel bad," I said to Kevin. "You're a tough guy, but there's always somebody tougher."

"She didn't beg me," Kevin said, "we'd still be at it."

"Sure," I said. "Now, do you, Kate, love him, Kevin?"

"Yes."

"Do you, Kevin, love her, Kate?"

"For crissake, what's it look like? Of course I do."

"You ever hit her?" I said.

"Once."

"Hit her once, or on one occasion hit her a number of times?"

"Just once, total," Kevin said.

He didn't want to look at me. He didn't like me knocking him on his kazoo in front of his girlfriend.

"That right, Kate?"

"Yes. He hit me on the arm, up near the shoulder."

"I was drunk," Kevin said. "And she was driving me crazy."

"About what?" I said.

"About her freakin' job. That bitch she works for doesn't want me around her."

"I need that job," Kate said. "How'm I going to eat, I don't have that job?"

"I'll be working again, goddammit, I'm just between right now."

"What do you do when you work?" I said.

"Heavy equipment. Company I worked for went outta business. I'll hook on someplace pretty quick."

"That the way you understand it, Kate?" I said.

"Yes. I know he'll get another job. But we need to eat now."

"We?"

"Kevin and I," Kate said.

I looked at him. He didn't look back.

"You supporting him?" I said.

"Just for now," she said. "I give him a little money."

"That right?" I said to Kevin.

"Yeah."

"He'd do it for me," she said.

"And when he shows up while you're walking the baby, he's not stalking you?"

"It's the only chance we get," Kevin said.

"Except we always fight," Kate said.

"Because he wants you to leave your job, and you don't want to."

"Not until he's on his feet again."

I walked a few feet and stood at the riverbank and looked at the gray water. Behind me the two of them sat on the bench as if they were waiting outside the principal's office. After a while I spoke to them without turning around.

"Why don't you get another job, Kate? Where the boss is a little more flexible."

"That's what I keep fucking telling her," Kevin said.

"I don't have time to look," Kate said. "And . . ."

"And?"

"And it's the baby. I love her. I want to take care of her. Nobody else wants to take care of her. I . . . I don't want her to grow up to be like her mother."

There were some sailboats skittering about erratically on the basin, driven inconsistently by the wind off the land. I watched them for a while. Then I walked back to where Kevin and Kate sat on the bench.

"Okay," I said. "Kate, you'll have to save another kid from her mother, and let a new nanny save Miranda."

"How am I going to get another job?"

"I'm going to get you one, and Kevin too."

"I can get my own job," Kevin said.

"Yeah sure, you're tough as nails and proud as a peacock. Which, so far, has enabled you to screw yourself up with the woman you love."

"You think I'm not tough 'cause you got a lucky punch in?"

"We both know it wasn't lucky," I said. "I can help you, unless you insist on being an asshole."

"You really think you can get us both jobs?" Kate said.

"It's a booming economy," I said.

She nodded and looked at Kevin. He smiled at her.

"You want to do this?" he said.

"Yes."

"Then we'll do it," he said.

TWENTY-FIVE

I WAS IN my office on Wednesday morning, eating some sugared donuts and drinking coffee and reading the paper. Wednesdays were always promising, because Susan didn't see patients on Wednesdays. She taught in the morning and normally spent the rest of the day with me.

And morning was always a good part of the day. I had the paper to read. The streets were full of people, fresh-showered and dressed well and heading for work. My office was still. The coffee was recent. The donuts were everything donuts should be, and the bright beginning of the day contained the prospect of unlimited possibility. When I had finished the paper, I put my feet up and dragged the phone over, and called Vinnie Morris.

"Gino do business with any construction companies?" I said.

"Of course," Vinnie said.

"I got a heavy-equipment operator looking for work."

"He connected?" Vinnie said.

"He's connected to me," I said. "Can you get him hired?"

"Sure," Vinnie said.

"Quickly?" I said.

"Tomorrow?"

"That's quickly," I said.

"I'll get back to you," Vinnie said.

We hung up. I went to the window and looked down at Boylston Street where Berkeley intersected. A stream of good-looking professional women moved past. Their outfits were tailored and ironed and careful. I was too high to hear, but I knew that their high heels clicked on the warm pavement as they walked. And I knew most of them smelled of pretty good perfume. Had I been closer, they in turn would have noticed that I smelled fetchingly of Club Man. But there was no one to smell me . . . yet. I looked at my watch. Quarter to eleven. She'd be here in an hour and a half, or so she had promised. Punctuality was not Susan's strength. She always intended to be on time, but she seemed to have some kind of chronometric dyslexia, which thwarted her intent, nearly always. Had she been pre-dictably late, say fifteen minutes every time, then you could simply adjust your expectations. But she was sometimes a minute late and sometimes an hour late, and on rare and astonishing occasions, she was five minutes early. Since I had no way to gauge her coming hither or her going hence, I accepted the fact that readi-ness is all, and remained calm.

I poured the rest of the coffee into my cup and rinsed the pot out and threw the filter away, added a little milk and a lot of sugar to my cup, and sat back at my desk with my feet up. I sipped the coffee and thought about the Clives and Tedy Sapp and Polly Brown and Dalton Becker and came no closer to understanding what had happened than I had before I got canned.

The phone rang. It was Vinnie.

"Crocker Construction," he said. "Tell your guy to ask for Marty Rincone. Use my name."

"Where are they?" I said.

"Building condos on the beach in Revere. He'll see the trucks."

"Thank you," I said.

"You're welcome," Vinnie said. "You know where Hawk is?"

"France," I said.

"Working?"

"I don't think so. He went with a good-looking French professor from BC. Can I help you with something?"

"You could, but you won't."

"Okay, if I hear from Hawk, I'll tell him you were asking."

"Today or tomorrow, or don't bother. After that I'll have done it myself."

We hung up. Vinnie wasn't a chatty guy.

The mail came. I went through it. Nobody had sent me a check. Although one client had written a grateful letter. There were a couple of bills, for which I wrote a couple of checks. I threw away several offers to make my phone bills lower than a child molester.

Susan arrived. However late she might be, she was always worth the wait. Today she had on cropped white pants, and a striped shirt, and sneakers. I sensed that our afternoon would be informal. She sat on the couch and wrinkled her nose.

"Are you wearing Club Man again, or have they just painted the radiators?"

"You fear Club Man, don't you?" I said. "Because you're afraid that after just a single whiff, your libido will jump out of your psyche and begin to break-dance right here on the rug."

"That's probably it," she said. "Would you like to hear our plans for the rest of the day?"

"Yes, but first I need to find work for a nanny," I said.

"A nanny," Susan said.

"Yes."

I told her about Kate and Kevin and Valerie and Miranda.

"Things are not always as they appear," Susan said.

"You've noticed that too," I said.

"I'm a trained psychologist," Susan said. "You've gotten Kevin a job already?"

"Yep. Through Vinnie Morris."

"I'm not sure I have Vinnie's clout."

"Thank God for that," I said.

"But I can ask around," Susan said. "Most of the women I know work."

"As do most of the men," I said.

"Your point, Mr. Politically Correct?"

"Could be a father needs a nanny," I said.

"I'll ask the men too," she said. "Now would you like to hear our plans for the day?"

"Do they involve heavy breathing?"

"Absolutely," Susan said. "Whenever I smell your cologne."

TWENTY-SIX

SUSAN FOUND KATE a job as a teacher's aide in a private nursery school in Cambridge. Kevin was welcomed at Crocker Construction, where everyone treated him very respectfully. A couple of days after Kate had quit, Valerie Hatch stalked into my office without closing the door behind her.

"What the hell kind of operation are you running here?" she said.

"No need for thanks," I said. "Just doing my job."

"You sonovabitch," she said. "Because of you I've lost my nanny."

"Glad to do it," I said.

"Do you have any idea what it is like to be a career woman with a child?"

"No."

"Well, maybe you'd like to try the fast track someday while you've got a sixteen-month-old kid clinging to your damned skirt."

"I don't think a skirt would improve my fast-track chances."

"Don't avoid the issue," she said.

"Ms. Hatch, there is no issue," I said. "Kate didn't want to work for you, so she quit and got another job."

"Which you helped her with."

"Yes."

"You even got a job for that lout of a boyfriend."

"I did," I said.

"That is not what I employed you for."

"I know," I said. "I quit too."

"Don't think I'm going to take this kind of betrayal passively."

"Okay," I said. "I won't think that."

"I have every intention of pursuing this with the appropriate licensing agency."

I nodded.

"And don't think I'm going to pay your bill."

"There is no bill," I said.

"You mean they bought you off?"

"I mean this is *pro bono*," I said. "Would you like to know what I think?"

"No."

"Few people do," I said.

We were quiet. She glared at me.

"Well, what is it?"

"What is what?"

"What you think," she said. "My God, you're a fool."

"I think you should hire a new nanny."

She stared at me.

"That's your idea?"

I smiled and nodded. She stared at me some more.

"Men!" she said, and turned and stomped out of my office.

TWENTY-SEVEN

It WAS A month or so after I had failed Valerie Hatch so miserably. I was sitting in my office reading a book by Jonathan Lear about Freud and other things, when Dolly Hartman came into my office like an old sweet song and sat down in a client chair and crossed her spectacular legs.

"Do you remember me?" she said.

"Yes, I do. How are you, Ms. Hartman?"

"Please call me Dolly."

She was wearing a print summer dress and white high heels and no stockings. Her legs were the regulation horse-country tan. She was iridescent with cool sexuality that made me want to run around the desk and ask to die in her arms.

"You're looking well," I said. It was a weak substitute but it preserved my dignity.

"Thank you," she said. "Is that a good book?"

"I don't know," I said. "I don't understand it."

"Oh, I bet you do."

"Just the easy parts," I said.

We smiled at each other.

"What brings you to Boston?" I said, listening to my voice, hoping it wasn't hoarse.

"I wanted to see you," she said, and shifted a little in her chair and crossed her legs the other way. Which displayed a fair amount of thigh. I observed closely. You never knew when a clue might present itself.

She smiled. I cleared my throat.

"How are things in Lamarr?" I said.

Spenser, conversationalist par excellence.

"That's why I wanted to see you," she said. "Things are hideous in Lamarr."

I decompressed a little. She wasn't just there to flash her thighs at me. Not that I don't like thighs. Had that been her purpose, she'd have been welcome. But because she was there with a problem, I could start acting like it was a business call, which would dilute my impulse to bugle like a moose.

"Tell me about it," I said.

"There's something very wrong at Three Fillies," Dolly said.

"Like what?"

"Well, neither my son nor I have any access."

"Access?"

"We're not allowed in," she said. "Not the stables. Not the house. Nowhere."

"What happens if you go and ask to be let in?" I said.

"The security guards prevent us."

"At the house too?"

"Yes."

"Security South?" I said.

"Yes."

"Any explanation?"

"No. Simply that they have their orders."

"Have you called Penny?"

"She won't take my calls."

"Stonie? SueSue?"

"They don't answer or return my calls."

"There any progress on Walter's murder?" I said.

"None."

"Any more horses?"

"No."

"You talk to Becker about this?"

"The sheriff?"

"Un-huh."

"I can't discuss this sort of thing with some policeman."

"Oh."

"I wish to hire you," she said.

"To do what?"

"To find out what happened to Walter Clive."

"What can I do that the cops can't do?"

"You can report to me," she said. "And maybe you won't pussyfoot around the Clive family quite as much as the local police."

"That may be," I said. "But if they don't want to talk to me, they don't have to."

"They have shut themselves off, since Walter's death. They have shut me out. They have shut my son out."

"Are you in Walter Clive's will?" I said.

She was silent for a time. I waited. She crossed her legs the other way. Which gave me something to do while I waited.

"Why do you ask?" she said.

"I'm a nosy guy," I said.

She was silent again. I waited some more.

"I was supposed to be," she said.

"And?"

"The attorneys tell me I'm not," she said.

"How long were you with him?" I said.

"Eight years."

"Did he say he'd take care of you?"

"Of course."

"Do you feel there was chicanery?"

"God, don't you talk funny," she said.

"It's not my fault," I said. "I've been sleeping with a Harvard Ph.D."

She smiled. Her teeth were perfectly even and absolutely white. The effect was dazzling, even though I suspected orthodontic intervention.

"I've done that," she said.

"Hopefully not with the same one," I said.

"Hopefully," she said.

"Do you think somebody doctored the will to cut you out?" I said.

"I don't know what to think," she said. "I don't mean to come off sounding greedy, but . . . I . . ."

She shifted a little in her chair and crossed her legs again. She seemed to sit up a little straighter.

"I am what would have been called, in more genteel times, a courtesan. I have been not only the sex partner but the companion and support of several powerful men, of whom Walter Clive was the most recent."

"Did any of the others stiff you?"

"None of the others have died," she said. "But each made a financial settlement with me when our relationship ended. I know Walter would have done the same thing, if we had parted before his death. None of these arrangements were about love. But in each instance we liked each other, and we understood what we were doing."

"Are you okay financially?"

"Yes. I am quite comfortable, and I shall almost certainly establish a, ah, liaison with another powerful and affluent man."

"So hiring me is a thirst for justice," I said.

"I want my son's inheritance."

"You think Walter Clive should have left money to your son."

"Our son," Dolly said.

"Yours and Walter's?"

"Yes."

"Does your son know this?" I said.

"Not yet."

"Did Walter know this?"

"I told him. We agreed that Walter would undergo some DNA testing."

"Did he?"

"I don't know."

"He died without telling you."

"Yes."

"You and Walter have been together eight years," I said. "Your son, Jason?"

"Yes."

"Jason appears to be in his middle twenties," I said.

She smiled again.

"The eight years is public and official," she said. "Our liaison began a long time before that, while Walter was still married to the beatnik."

"Sherry Lark?"

"I became pregnant with Jason about the same time she did with Stonie. I said nothing. I knew better than to upset the apple cart at that time. I ended the relationship with Walter, and went away and had Jason, and raised him. Later when the beatnik was gone, I came back into his life. I never explained Jason, and Walter never asked."

"Did they ever divorce?"

"Walter and the beatnik?"

"Yes."

"No, they didn't."

"Why not?"

"I think each hated the other too much to give in," Dolly said.

"Why didn't you tell Clive about Jason when you came back?"

"The separation was horrible. The beatnik may be primarily interested in flowers and peace, but she tried to gouge him for every penny. Had she learned of Jason, she would have succeeded."

"And that would have been less for you," I said.

"And Jason," she said.

"What made you change your mind?" I said.

"Walter was revising his will. I wanted Jason to get

what was his. No one would have to know anything until Walter's death, and then Miss Hippie Dippie couldn't do anything about it."

"And Walter wanted proof that Jason was actually his son," I said. "Hence the DNA tests."

"Yes."

"Where was he tested?"

"I don't know."

"Was Jason tested?"

"We donated some blood for the DNA match. I spoke to our doctor first. Larry Klein. He's a lovely man. Very cute. Jason just thought it was part of a routine physical."

"Do you think the rest of the family knows anything?" I said.

"To my knowledge, you and I are the only ones who know about this, and of course Dr. Klein."

"You know he went to Dr. Klein?"

"No. He said he had. And was waiting for the results."

"You're sure Clive is Jason's father?" I said.

"I said I was a courtesan. I am not a whore."

We sat for a while. I thought about the offer. The case had its own merits, and it was also a wedge back into the situation. It is very bad for business when someone kills your client. I might see Penny again, whom I liked. I would almost certainly get a further look at Dolly's knees, which I also liked.

"Georgia in August," I said. "Hot dog!"

TWENTY-EIGHT

- -

IT WAS HOT in Lamarr. The sky was cloudless and the sun hammered down through the thick air. I parked at the top of the long driveway. Everything was pretty much the same. The lawn was still smooth and green. The sprinklers still worked, separating small rainbows out of the hot sunlight. On the wide veranda in the shade, two guys in Security South uniforms stood looking at me. As I got out of my car one of them walked down the front steps and over to me. He was carrying a clipboard.

"Your name, sir?"

"Spenser," I said. "Nice clipboard."

"I don't see your name here, sir."

"With an S-p-e-n-*s*-e-r," I said. "Like the English poet."

"I still don't see it, sir. Did you call ahead?"

"I certainly did."

"And who'd you speak with?"

"Some guy said his name was Duane."

"I can check with him, sir."

"Sure," I said.

He walked a few steps away, reached down and adjusted his radio, and spoke into a microphone clipped to his epaulet. Then he listened, readjusted his radio, and walked back to me.

"Duane says he informed you already that you're not welcome," the security guy said. He was a little less respectful when he said it. The other security guy, still on the veranda, came a couple of steps closer, though still in the shade, and let his hand rest on his holstered weapon.

"I know," I said. "But I'm sure he didn't mean it."

"He meant it."

"Does Penny know I'm here?"

"Miss Clive doesn't want to see you."

"How disheartening," I said. "Stonie? SueSue?"

"Nobody wants to see you, pal. Including me. I'm sick of talking to you."

"I knew you were trouble," I said, "the minute I saw your clipboard."

"Beat it."

He pointed a finger at my car. I nodded and got in and started up.

"There's more than one way to skin a cat," I said.

Unfortunately I couldn't think what it was, so I rolled up my window, turned the a/c up, backed slowly down the long driveway to the street, and drove back into town to talk with Becker.

He was at his desk in the sheriff's substation in Lamarr, drinking Coca-Cola from one of those twenty-ounce plastic bottles shaped like the original glass ones.

"You remember the original bottles," I said when I sat down.

"Yep. Glass, six ounces."

"And then Pepsi came along and doubled the amount for the same price."

Becker grinned.

"Twice as much," he said, "for a nickel too, Pepsi-Cola is the drink for you."

"And nothing's been the same since," I said.

Becker shrugged.

"Shit happens," he said. "What are you doing back in town?"

"I have a client."

"Really?"

"Yep."

"Who?"

"Dolly Hartman."

"She want you to find out who killed Walter?"

"Yep."

"Thinks we can't?"

"Notices you haven't," I said.

Becker nodded, sipped some Coke.

"Not much to go on," he said. "Plus the Clives have buttoned up tight."

"I know. I went out there. Couldn't get in."

"Well, I can get in, but it doesn't do me any good. Nobody says anything."

"Dolly implied that you might be walking a little light around the Clives because they're connected."

"Dolly's right. I'm appointed by the sheriff. But the

sheriff ain't appointed by anyone. He gets elected, and that takes money."

"And the Clives have a lot of it."

"You bet," Becker said.

"You getting some pressure?"

"Un-huh."

"Between you and me," I said. "You got any thought who killed Clive?"

"You used to be a cop," Becker said. "When a rich guy dies, who's first on the list?"

"His heirs," I said.

"Un-huh."

"Any more horses been killed?" I said.

"Nope."

"You think there's a connection?"

"I wasn't getting pressure, might be something I could look into."

"I'm not getting any pressure," I said.

"Yet," Becker said.

"What do you know about Security South?" I said.

"Just what I already told you."

"Is what you told me something you know or something they told you?"

"Something they told me," Becker said. "At the time, I had no reason to look into it."

"And now?"

"Next year's an election year."

"Not for me," I said.

"Look," Becker said. "I'm a pretty good cop, I do say so. But I got a wife never worked a day in her life, I got a few years left until I'm eligible for a pension, I got a daughter in Memphis I send money to pretty regular. You bring me stuff that can't be ignored, I won't ignore it."

He picked up his Coke, and drained the bottle and put it back down slowly on his desk.

"Can you say 'stalking-horse'?" I said.

Becker almost smiled.

"Best I can do," he said.

TWENTY-NINE

THE BATH HOUSE Bar and Grill was jumping. It was crowded with couples dancing, couples sitting at tables with their heads close together. The bar was packed two or three deep. Tedy Sapp was at his table, alone, drinking coffee. As I pushed through the crowd, people moved out of my way. Those who looked at me did so without affection.

"Back again," Sapp said as I sat down across from him. "You're not a quitter."

"New client," I said.

A waiter came by and poured Sapp some coffee. He looked at me. I shook my head.

"Nothing to drink?"

"Long day," I said. "It'll make me sleepy."

Sapp glanced around the room.

"What do you think of the scene?" he said.

"Not my scene," I said.

"It bother you?"

"Nope."

Sapp looked at me for a time.

"Nothing much does," he said, "does it?"

"Way the patrons acted when I came in, I figure I'm not their scene, either."

Sapp grinned.

"You don't look like a gay guy," Sapp said.

"Neither do you," I said.

"I know. That's why I do the hair color. Trying to gay up a little."

"You got a partner?"

"Yep."

"What's he do?"

"Ophthalmologist."

"So you're not looking to meet somebody."

"No," Sapp said.

"So what's the difference?"

"It's important if you're gay, to be gay. Especially me, who was straight so long, my, what would I call it, my, ah, constituency is more at ease if I'm identifiably gay."

"And the blond hair does it?"

"It's pretty much all I can do. I still look like something from the World Wrestling Federation. But it's better than nothing."

"Works for me, Blondie," I said. "You know anything about the Clive family that you didn't know last time we talked?"

"They seem to be cleaning house," Sapp said.

"How so?"

"Kicked old Cord out on his ass," Sapp said.

"Stonie divorcing him?"

"Don't know."

"Where's Cord now?"

"In town somewhere. I can find out."

"Be obliged," I said.

Sapp got up and began to work his way through the room, stopping occasionally to talk with someone. I watched the smoke gather up near the ceiling of the low room. It seemed to me on casual observation that gay men smoked more than straight men. But I was probably working with too small a sample. All I could really say was that a number of these gay men smoked more than I did. The ceiling fan turned slowly in the smoke, moving it about in small eddies, doing nothing to dispel it. The jukebox was very loud. I had a brief third-person vision of myself, sitting alone and alien in a gay bar, a thousand miles from home, with the smoke hanging above me, and music I didn't like pounding in my ears.

Sapp came back and sat down.

"Cord's bunking in with his brother-in-law," Sapp said.

He handed me a matchbook.

"I wrote down the address for you."

"Brother-in-law?" I said.

"Yeah, Pud. I guess he got the boot too."

"Pud and Cord?" I said. "Getting the boot makes strange bedfellows."

"I guess it do," Sapp said. "Who's your client?"

I shook my head.

"Never get in trouble keeping your mouth shut," Sapp said.

I nodded. Sapp sipped some of his coffee, holding the cup in both hands, looking over the rim, his gaze moving slowly back and forth across the room.

"You married?" Sapp said.

"Not exactly," I said.

"Separated?"

"Nope. I'm with somebody. But we're not married."

"You love her?"

"More than the spoken word can tell," I said.

"You live together?"

"No."

"You love her, but you're not married and you don't live together. Why not?"

"Seems to work best for us this way."

Sapp shrugged.

"You fool around?" he said.

"No. You?"

"No."

"You think Pud and Cord are a couple," I said, "or just orphans of the storm?"

"Far as I know, neither one of them could make a living on his own," Sapp said. "Now that they don't have the Clive tit to nurse on, I figure they're splitting the rent."

Sapp's slow surveillance of the room stopped and focused. I followed his glance. Three men stood inside the door. Two of them were large, the third was tall, high-shouldered, and skinny. The large ones looked fat but not soft. None of them looked like they had come in to dance. Without a word Sapp got up and moved softly toward them, his hands loose at his sides, his shoulders bowed a little forward. One of the big guys had a red plastic mesh baseball cap on backwards, the little adjustable plastic strap across his forehead just above his eyebrows. The other man was fatter, wearing a white tank top, his fat arms red with sunburn. The three men stood close together at the door, looking around and giggling among themselves. They were drunk.

The tall skinny one with the high shoulders yelled into the room. "Any you sissy boys want to fight?"

Sapp stopped in front of the three men.

" 'Fraid I'm going to have to ask you boys to leave," he said gently.

"Who the fuck are you?" the skinny one said.

"My name's Tedy Sapp."

As he spoke Sapp moved slightly closer so that the skinny one had to back up slightly or risk being bumped.

"Well, we got as much right as anybody else to come in here and have us a couple pops," the guy in the baseball hat said.

"No. Just step back out, gentlemen, same door you came in, there'll be no trouble."

"Trouble," said the guy in the hat. "Who's going to give us trouble? You?"

"Yep," Sapp said. "It'll be me."

He brought his hands up slowly and rubbed them together thoughtfully in front of his chest, the fingertips touching his chin.

"I never met no fag could tell me what to do, pal. I want a drink."

"Not here," Sapp said.

"We getting us a fucking drink or we going to kick a lot of fag ass," the guy in the hat said.

"Not here," Sapp said.

The guy with the hat said, "Fuck you," and tried to push by Sapp. Sapp hit him with the side of his left hand in the throat, and hit the skinny guy on the hinge of the jaw with the side of his clenched right hand. The guy in the tank top backed up a couple of steps. Sapp began punching, not like a fighter but like a martial arts guy, both fists from the shoulder, feet evenly spaced and balanced. He hit the guy in the hat maybe three times and swiveled a half-turn and hit the skinny guy two more. Both men went down. Tank Top looked at Sapp and then looked at me. I realized that I had moved up beside Sapp. Tank Top helped his companions to their still-shaky feet.

"No trouble," he said.

"None at all," Sapp said.

Tank Top guided his pals out in front of him and the door swung shut behind them. Sapp looked at me and grinned.

"Planning to jump in?" he said.

"No need," I said. "You have learned well, grasshopper."

THIRTY

I WENT TO see Rudolph Vallone, the lawyer for the Clive estate, who also represented Dolly Hartman. He had a suite of offices upstairs in a Civil War–era brick building next to the courthouse, right on the square in the middle of Lamarr, where he could look out his window at the pyramid of cannonballs and the statue of the Confederate soldier that grounded the town in the lost glory of its past.

Vallone sat in the biggest of the several offices, at a desk in front of a Palladian window with the best view of the cannonballs. He had on a gray seersucker suit and a very bright floral tie. His white hair was long and brushed back. His white Vandyke beard was neatly trimmed, and there was about his person the faint aura of bay rum and good cigars and satisfying fees.

"Nice to see you again, Mr. Spenser. I recall you from the funeral."

I'd met him very perfunctorily. One point for Rudy.

"I was wondering if you could tell me a little about Walter Clive's estate," I said.

"Well, you're direct enough, aren't you."

"You bet," I said.

"In all honesty, Mr. Spenser, I'd need to know a little more about why you're asking, and a little more specifically what you want to know."

"Of course you would," I said. "What would be the point of law school if you didn't."

He smiled.

"I'm representing Dolly Hartman," I said. "I wish to know who benefits from Clive's will."

"Why, for God's sake, man, I'm Dolly's attorney. She has only to ask me directly."

"She asked me to ask you directly," I said.

"I don't know that."

"No, nor should you care a hell of a lot. We both know if I want to go to a little trouble I can find this out. It's a matter of public record."

"So why come to me?"

"You're closer," I said.

He smiled a wide smile, a good old Georgia boy, friendly as lemon cake.

"But not necessarily easier," he said.

"And there are things I want to know that may not be a matter of public record," I said.

"I don't see how I can help you," he said.

"You represented Walter Clive?"

"Yes."

"And now you represent the Clive estate."

"I do."

"You represent Dolly as well," I said.

"I just told you I do."

"Dolly feels that the estate is screwing her and her son."

"She's never said that to me."

"She claims she has."

"Spenser, you better understand some things about Dolly," Vallone said. "She is not one to miss anything she sees as the main chance."

"So if this ends up in court, are you going to be attorney for both sides?"

"It won't end up in court."

"It might, or I might boogie on up to Atlanta and talk with the Georgia Bar Association."

"Don't be ridiculous."

"It makes people laugh when I mention it," I said. "But the bar association has an ethics committee."

"I'm perfectly aware," he said, "of the bar association. My efforts in this case have been motivated solely by the best interests of everyone involved."

"So who are Clive's heirs? The three daughters?"

Vallone dipped his head a little in some kind of acknowledgment.

"Yes," he said.

"Solely."

"Yes."

"Was he planning to rewrite his will, or in the process of it, or any such thing?"

"No."

"Never mentioned looking out for Dolly or her son?"

"Her son?" Vallone said. "I understand why he might

have taken care of Dolly, but the son rendered him no service."

"Dolly says he was Clive's son as well."

"Walter Clive's son? That's absurd. The boy is in his middle twenties. Walter was only with Dolly for, what, eight or ten years."

"There's a story there, but it doesn't matter."

"I'd be happy to listen."

"In all honesty, Mr. Vallone, I'd need to know a little more about why you're asking, and a little more specifically what you want to know."

Vallone let his chair lean forward. He opened a cigar humidor. He offered me one, and I shook my head. He selected one slightly smaller than a Little League bat and snipped it and lit it and leaned back and smoked it for a minute. Then he laughed.

"By God, sir," he said. "Just, goddamned, by God."

THIRTY-ONE

I HAD BREAKFAST with Dr. Larry Klein at the hospital cafeteria at six in the morning.

"I'm sorry to be so early," he said when I sat down, "but I have rounds at six-thirty and patients all day."

"I don't mind," I said. "Maybe I'll catch a worm."

Klein was older than I was expecting. He was smallish and wiry and looked like he might have been the off guard at a small college who got by on his set shot. I had juice, coffee, and a corn muffin. Klein was eating two frosted sweet rolls that would have sickened a coyote.

"You represent Dolly Hartman?" he said.

"Yes."

"I like Dolly," he said.

He put most of a pat of butter on one of his sweet rolls.

"Me too," I said. "Were you her physician as well as Walter Clive's?"

"Yes."

"Did Walter Clive undergo DNA testing?"

Klein sat back a little and looked at me. Around me, in the small cafeteria, nurses and patients and bleary-eyed interns were shuffling along the food line, loading up on stuff that would challenge the vascular system of a Kenyan marathoner. I could almost hear the arteries clogging all over the room. If Klein heard them he didn't seem worried.

"Why do you ask?" Klein said.

"I'd heard he was trying to establish a question of paternity."

Klein ate some of his sweet roll, and chewed thoughtfully, and drank some coffee and wiped his mouth on his napkin.

"I'm thinking about ethics," he said.

"Always nice to find someone who does," I said.

"If I may ask," Klein said, "what is the, ah, thrust of your question?"

"Dolly Hartman says that Jason is Walter's son. I thought if it was true, it might help me to find out who killed Walter."

"I don't see how."

"Well, with all due respect, Doctor, you probably don't have to see how. But in the murder of a wealthy person, it's good to eliminate all the heirs."

Klein nodded. He buttered his second sweet roll.

"Yes, I can see how it would help. Is Jason mentioned in Walter's will?"

"Apparently not," I said.

Klein swallowed some sweet roll and drank the remainder of his coffee and looked at his watch.

"I'm going to get some more coffee," he said. "Care for any?"

"This is fine," I said.

Klein got up and went to the counter. I looked around at the room, which was painted with some sort of horse-country scene of riders in red coats, and dogs and rolling countryside. Klein came back with more coffee and sat down. I smiled at him. Friendly as a guy selling siding. He drank some coffee and set the cup down and looked at me. I waited.

"They were father and son," Klein said.

"Who knows that?"

"Me."

"You haven't told anyone?"

"I told Walter. No one else has asked until you."

"You didn't tell Dolly? Or her kid?"

"I was, to tell you the truth, uncertain as to what my responsibility was. I have worried at it every day until now. In a way I'm glad you showed up."

"Was Clive secretive about the test?" I said.

"Very. He took it under a pseudonym."

"And you've told no one."

"No. Why?"

"Christ, I don't know," I said. "I barely know what to ask, let alone what the answers mean."

Klein smiled. "Rather like the practice of medicine," he said.

"I don't want to hear that," I said.

"Well, it's not always true," he said.

"When the time comes, I will tell Dolly and Jason about the DNA results," I said. "But in the meantime I think we should shut up about it."

"Fine with me," Klein said. "Even in death, a patient has the right to privacy. But why do you care?"

"I'm looking for a guy who murdered someone. Anything that I know that he doesn't know is to my benefit."

Klein swallowed some more coffee. "And if the murder had something to do with the inheritance, this information might be dangerous."

"To someone," I said.

"Maybe even to him who holds it," Klein said.

"Pretty smart for an internist," I said.

"Occasionally. Mostly I'm just trying to shag the nurses."

"Be my approach," I said.

Klein looked at his watch again. "Time for rounds," he said. "If I can help, I will. I liked Walter Clive."

THIRTY-TWO

PUD POTTER'S APARTMENT was down a side street off the square, past a sandwich shop and a place that sold baseball cards and used CDs. Upstairs, in the back, with a nice view of the railroad tracks. In the little front hall, I had to step over a narrow mattress on the floor. Beyond it there was just a bedroom, kitchenette, and bath. A window air conditioner was cranking as hard as it could, but the room wasn't cool. The mattress was bare except for a pillow and a slept-under green spread. The bed in the bedroom was unmade, but at least there were sheets. The walls were painted beige. The woodwork was painted brown. There were dishes in the sink in the kitchenette, and a couple of damp-looking towels littered the bathroom floor. Pud and Cord sat on the unmade bed while we talked. I leaned against the wall. They hadn't been awake long.

"Hard times," I said.

"Pathetic, is what it is," Pud said.

He wore a sleeveless undershirt and jeans. He had weight lifters' arms and a boozer's gut. Cord sat next to him in a pair of tennis shorts and no shirt.

"Things moved pretty swiftly," Cord said. "Take us a little time to get our feet under us."

"And do fucking what?" Pud said.

"Get on with our lives," Cord said.

"Neither one of us knows how to do shit," Pud said. "All we did was service the women, and you weren't even any good at that."

"I don't know what you're talking about," Cord said.

"You think he don't know?" Pud said. "He knows. Don't you know?"

I said, "Sure."

"I ever have any trouble with you?" Pud said.

"No, never," I said. "We were fooling around once at a party at the Clive place. But no trouble."

Pud nodded.

"I drink too much," he said. "Makes it hard to remember sometimes. I know I can be a damn fool."

"Lot of that going around," I said.

"What do you know?" Cord said.

"About what?"

"About me."

Somehow the air conditioner had succeeded in making the room clammy but not cool.

"I know you are gay. I know you prefer boys to men. I know your wife was working truck stops."

Cord looked at the floor.

"See," Pud said. "I told you he knew."

Cord shook his head slightly, still looking down.

"What's the thing about truck stops?" Pud said.

"Cord can tell you," I said.

"I don't know anything about it," Cord said.

He sat motionless. His voice was very small.

"She'd have made sure you knew," I said.

"Knew what?" Pud said.

Cord began to cry softly. Pud stared at him and then at me.

"Who said what? What's the matter?"

Cord continued to cry quietly. Pud put one arm around his shoulder.

"Come on," he said, "come on now, Cord."

Cord turned his face in against Pud's shoulder and sobbed. Pud's face reddened and his body stiffened, but he kept his arm where it was. He didn't look at me.

"What's going to happen to us?" Cord mumbled against Pud's shoulder.

"We're gonna be fine," Pud said. "We just need a little time to get our feet under us, you know. We're all right. We'll meet somebody else. We'll be all right."

I waited.

"Cord's real sensitive," Pud said. "They're like that."

The room was too small. The air was too close. The emotions were too raw. I felt claustrophobic.

"I'll buy breakfast," I said.

Pud nodded.

"Some coffee," he said. "Coffee'll make us feel better."

"You take a shower," he said to Cord, "and get dressed. We'll meet you at Finney's."

He looked at me.

"Joint downstairs," he said. "They got a couple booths."

He patted Cord's shoulder once and stood up and led me out of the apartment. Cord was still sitting on the bed sniffling.

There were in fact two booths in Finney's sandwich shop. We sat in the second one. It was against the back wall, opposite the counter, where a man and a woman were eating scrambled eggs and grits, and a grill man was busy at his trade. The young woman who worked the counter had a bright blond helmet of big hair. She also worked the booths. When she came over, with her hair and her order pad, Pud requested orange juice, ham, eggs over easy, grits, toast, and coffee. I settled for coffee.

"Poor bastard," Pud said.

"Cord?"

"Yeah. I mean I knew, we all knew, that he was a chicken fucker. Walt had to bail his ass out a couple times. And we all figured he wasn't fucking Stonie."

The waitress brought Pud's juice, and coffee for both of us.

"I mean he's queer as a square donut."

"Stonie knew it too," I said.

"Sure."

"What kept them together?" I said.

Pud drank his orange juice in one long pull, and put the empty glass down.

"How the fuck do I know? I wasn't a pretty good linebacker, I'd a flunked outta Alabama my freshman year. It was like he was okay as long as she was taking care of him."

"So why'd she stop?"

"Taking care of him?"

"Yeah."

Pud did a big shrug.

"Fucking Clive raised some weird daughters," he said.

"Tell me about it."

The waitress came with Pud's breakfast. He ate some of it before he spoke again.

"After Walt died, everything got really funky around there. I don't know exactly what was going on, but the girls were spending a lot of time together."

"Stonie and SueSue?"

"And Penny. They'd go down to the barn office and shut the door, and be in there a long time."

He ate a bite of ham.

"Then one day SueSue gives me a call at the business office and asks me to come down to the barn. I do, and she's there and so is Stonie and Cord, and Penny and that jerkoff Delroy. Penny's sitting behind the desk, and she's as nice as pie, but she tells us we gotta leave. That we are no longer welcome on Clive property."

He ate some egg, pushing it onto his fork with a piece of toast, and drank some coffee, and gestured at the blond counter girl for more coffee.

"And I say, 'For crissake, I'm married to a Clive.' And Penny says, 'That will be taken care of.' And I'm looking at SueSue and she's not looking at me. And I see Cord staring at Stonie, and she's not looking at him either. They're both looking at Penny. And I say, 'Sue-Sue, for crissake, what is this?' And she shakes her head and won't look at me, and Penny says, 'It is too painful for my sisters, I'll talk.' "

The man and woman at the counter finished breakfast, left a dollar tip, and walked out of the shop. The blond waitress scooped the tip.

"So I say, 'I'll be fucked if you're gonna just run me off like a stray dog.' And Penny nods, and she's so nice, she says, 'I have asked Mr. Delroy to see to it.' And Delroy says, 'You have until Monday.' And . . .' " Pud spread his hands and raised his shoulders. "That's it. Monday Delroy and four guys show up at my house and walk me off the property with nothing I couldn't pack in a suitcase."

"Is it your house?"

"Do I own it? No. It's on Clive property. Walt owned it. Same for Cord's place. Walt owned everything."

"You and SueSue having trouble?"

"No more than we ever had."

"When you had trouble, was it about drinking?"

"Yeah. She was right, I drank too much."

"I noticed when we were . . . fooling around at the party that night, she urged you to fight me."

"Yeah, she liked that. She liked to see me be a tough guy."

"Is that why you acted the part?"

"When I was drunk, sure. I mean, here I am living off her old man in her old man's house. I needed to show her I was worth something."

"She get on you about living off her father?"

"Nope. I think she liked it."

"Control?" I said.

He shrugged.

"I ain't a smart guy," he said.

"She faithful to you?" I said.

"Far as I know."

He was right. He wasn't a smart guy.

"But you fooled around."

"I never cheated on her with anyone she knew," he said. "Just some whores. I treated her with respect."

"That's why you kept the apartment."

"Yeah."

"SueSue knew about that?"

"Not from me," he said.

"SueSue drink a lot?" I said.

"We both liked a cocktail," he said.

"How did Cord react to all this?"

"In the barn office, when we got . . . fired, he never said a word, just kept staring at Stonie. Like his mother was leaving him."

"And afterwards?"

"After the barn office he just disappeared and the next time I saw him he's knocking at my apartment door. He looked like shit. Said he'd been sleeping in the back room of a queer bar."

"Bath House Bar and Grill," I said.

"Yeah."

"How'd he know where to come?" I said.

"I let him use the place every once in a while."

"For romantic interludes?"

"Whatever."

"You and Cord seem an unlikely pair," I said.

"Yeah. Me pals with a fairy. But you know, we were both in the same boat, coupla pet spaniels."

He ate the last of his breakfast.

THIRTY-THREE

CORD CLEANED UP well. When he joined us, showered, shampooed, clean-shaven, smelling of an under-
stated cologne, and casually dressed, he looked like a
successful broker on his day off. He slid into the booth
beside me and smiled pleasantly.

"Sorry I sort of slopped over up there. I've been under some stress."

The waitress came over, filled our coffee cups, and
asked Cord if he wanted anything to eat.

"You have any bran flakes?" Cord said.

She shook her head.

"Lunch menu," she said. "It's after eleven."

"Oh. All right, could I have some toast please, and a
cup of tea?"

"Tea?"

"Yes please, with lemon."

"Sure."

The waitress went off. Cord smiled at us brightly.

"You boys talked things out," he said.

"Relentlessly," I said. "Why do you think your wife suddenly ended your marriage?"

"Must we?" Cord said.

"We must."

"Well, as you've heard Pud suggest, albeit coarsely, our marriage was in some ways a sham. I was able to . . ." He paused, thinking how to say it. "Service her, I guess. But in more nontraditional ways."

"Okay, you were sexually mismatched," I said. "You both must have known that for a long time."

"Yes. I had hoped when we married that I could make a go of it, but . . ."

"But you couldn't get it up," Pud said.

Cord looked a little embarrassed. I assumed it was the language rather than the fact.

"Well, you did make a go, after all," I said. "How long have you been married?"

"Eight years."

"Any good ones?"

"Sex aside, yes. Stonie and I were pretty good friends."

"I'm not sure there is a sex aside," I said. "But why now?"

"Why did we break up now?"

"Yes."

The waitress returned with a cup of hot water, a tea bag, and toast with a pat of butter on each slice and a couple of little packets of grape jelly on the side. Pud said yes to more coffee. I said no.

"You got some kinda pie over there?" Pud said.

"Peach," she said.

"I'll have a slice. No sense drinking all this coffee without no pie."

The waitress smiled automatically and went for the pie. Cord dropped the tea bag in his hot water and jiggled it carefully.

"I've asked myself the same question," Cord said. "And it always comes back to Penny."

I waited. He jogged his tea bag, checking the color of the tea. The waitress came back and put a fork and a piece of pie down in front of Pud, put the check down beside it, and left. I picked up the check.

"Penny decided we should go," Cord said.

"Why did she?"

"I have no idea," Cord said. "You, Pud?"

"She never liked either one of us much," Pud said.

"I don't agree," Cord said. "She may have disapproved of you, Pud. All that boozing, and the macho business. But I thought Penny liked me."

"Guess you were wrong," Pud said.

"What do you guys know about Delroy?" I said.

"Pretty good guy," Pud said.

"A fascist bully," Cord said.

"How long has he worked for the Clive family?" I said.

"Before I showed up," Pud said.

"Yes," Cord said. "He was there when Stonie and I got married."

"Always security?"

"More or less," Cord said.

"He'd get me out of the trouble booze got me into,"

Pud said. "And he'd get Cord out of the trouble his dick got him into."

"What kind of trouble?" I said.

Pud ate the last bite of his pie. "Me? Drunk and disorderly. Soliciting sex from an undercover cop—the bitch. DWI. That kind of stuff."

"What did he do to fix it?"

"Hell, I don't know. I just know he'd come and get me from jail or whatever and bring me home and tell me to clean up my act. And I never heard about the charges again."

"You?" I said to Cord.

"He's done the same sort of thing for me," Cord said.

"Young boys?"

"Misunderstandings, really. At least one clear case of entrapment, in Augusta."

"Don't you hate when that happens," I said. "Delroy took care of it?"

"Yes. I assume acting on orders from Walter."

"Bribery?" I said. "Intimidation?"

"Both, I assume."

"And why don't you like him?"

"He was always so superior, so contemptuous. He's a classic homophobe."

"Aw hell, lotta people don't like homos," Pud said. "Don't make them fascists, for crissake."

Cord nibbled on his toast.

"Any other thoughts on Delroy?" I said.

"I think he's been humping Penny," Pud said.

I felt a little shock of anger, as if someone had said something insulting about Susan, though lower-voltage.

"Oh for God sakes, Pud, you always think everyone is humping everyone."

Pud shrugged.

"You out of the apartment for a while?" he said to Cord.

"Yes."

"Good. I gotta go clean up, I got a job interview."

"Where?" Cord said.

"Package delivery service. One of us gotta work."

"Good luck," Cord said.

"I get a job, maybe we can move out of the fucking phone booth we're in now," Pud said.

"I hope so," Cord said.

"See you around," Pud said to me. "Hope you make some progress."

I gave him my card.

"You think of anything," I said, "I'm at the Holiday Inn, right now, or you can call my office in Boston. I check my machine every day."

Pud took the card, gave me a thumbs-up, and left the sandwich shop.

"Did you know he's stopped drinking?" Cord said.

"No."

"Hasn't had a drink since this happened."

"Amazing."

"He's coarse and dreadfully incorrect, and not, I'm afraid, terribly bright," Cord said. "But my God, I don't know what I'd have done without him."

"People are often better sober," I said. "Do you think Delroy is humping Penny?"

"Well, I hadn't really thought about that, but she's

known him so long. I mean, what was she when Delroy came upon the scene, maybe fifteen?"

I waited while Cord tried to think about Delroy and Penny. This was hard for Cord. I was pretty sure he'd spent most of his life considering himself, and very little of his life considering anything else.

"I don't know," he said. "The idea seems sort of natural to me. I guess I'd have to say that if it proved so, I wouldn't be surprised by it."

"How about Stonie?" I said. "Do you think she was unfaithful?"

I knew the answer to that, though "unfaithful" didn't seem to quite fully cover truck-stop fellatio. I wanted to know if Cord knew.

"I would have understood," he said, "and I would have forgiven her, given how things were, and of course it's possible that she did things I don't know about. But no, I don't believe she was ever unfaithful."

"Hard to imagine," I said.

THIRTY-FOUR

THE LAMARR TOWN library was a two-and-a-half-block walk through the dense Georgia heat from the sandwich shop. By the time I got there my shirt was stuck to my back. The library was a white clapboard building, one story, with a long porch across the front. The porch roof was supported with some disproportionate white pillars. I went in. It was air-conditioned. I breathed for a while and then found an Atlanta phone book and looked up Security South. It had an address on Piedmont Road in Buckhead. Good neighborhood.

It took me two and a half hours to get to Atlanta and another twenty minutes to locate the Security South address on Piedmont in a small shopping center near the corner of East Paces Ferry Road. It was no cooler in Atlanta. When I got out of the car, the heat felt like it could be cut into squares and used to build a wall.

The little shopping center had a bookstore, a Thai restaurant, a hair salon, a place that sold bed linens and

bath accessories, and a storefront office with a sign on
the front window that read, "Bella's Business Services."
The more I looked, the more I didn't see Security South.
My best bet seemed to be Bella's, so I went in.

The room was cool and small and empty except for a
switchboard, a few office machines, two file cabinets, a
desk, a chair, and a woman. The woman was in the chair
behind the desk. She was black, with very short hair and
good shoulders.

"Bella?" I said.

"Denise," she said. "I bought the place from Bella."

"I'm looking for an outfit called Security South," I
said. "Which is listed at this address but does not seem
to be here."

"Right here," Denise said.

She was wearing a maroon linen dress with no
sleeves and her arms were strong-looking.

"Here?" I said.

"Yes, sir. If you'd like to leave a message, I can have
Mr. Delroy call you back."

"This is a mail drop," I said.

"And a phone service. We also do billing."

"Ah hah," I said.

"Ah hah?"

"Detectives say that when we come across a clue."

"Are you a detective?"

"I was beginning to wonder," I said. "I don't suppose
you could tell me who their clients are."

"No, sir, I'm sorry," Denise said. "But you can see
why we'd have to remain confidential about our customers."

"Sure," I said.

"You really a detective?" she said.

"Yep."

"Atlanta Police?"

"Boston. Private."

"A private eye?" she said. There was delight in her voice. "From Bahston?"

"Hey, do I make fun of your accent?" I said.

She smiled.

"Why, honey," she said, "we don't have no accent down here."

"Sho' 'nuff," I said.

I looked around the office. In the back, behind Denise's desk, was a window that opened onto a parking area. I could see the nose of what might have been a Honda Prelude parked behind the office. I smiled my aluminum-siding-salesman smile.

"While I'm here," I said, "you want me to check your security? I can give you a nice price on a beautiful system."

"No, thank you," she said. "I feel perfectly safe here."

"I meant an alarm system," I said. "Protect the office at night."

"From what? Somebody want to sneak in here and steal paper clips?"

"Well," I said, "I just assumed you had an alarm system. I could update it for you for cost, just cover the expense of my trip here."

"I don't have an alarm system," she said.

"I could put one in," I said. Always a plugger.

"Well, aren't you a hustler," Denise said.

"Well, you can't blame me for trying to salvage something," I said. "I don't find Security South, I don't get paid."

Denise smiled. She looked great when she smiled.

"No, I don't blame you, but I don't want anything you've got to sell."

"You're not the first woman to make that point," I said.

"I'm sure I'm not," Denise said. "You wish to leave a message for Mr. Delroy, I'll see that he gets it."

"Mr. Delroy?"

"Yessir, the CEO. Do you wish to leave a message for someone else?"

"No," I said. "No message."

"Best I can do," she said.

"Me too," I said, and smiled and opened her front door and wedged my way out into the swelter and thence to my car.

THIRTY-FIVE

THE POPULATION OF Atlanta is less than Boston's, but it is the center of a large region and for that it seems bigger. I was in the Buckhead neighborhood, north of Atlanta, where the governor lives, surrounded by large lawns, expensive houses, an upwardly mobile constituency, and some very good restaurants. One of them, Pano's and Paul's, was located out past the governor's mansion, in a small strip mall on West Paces Ferry Road. It was 5:35 when I got there, and there were tables available. I asked for one, got one, ordered an Absolut martini on the rocks and a deep-fried lobster tail, and tried to look like I preferred to dine alone in a fancy restaurant.

If Jon Delroy was the CEO of a security business that operated out of a file cabinet in Bella's Business Services, then how big an operation was it, and why was its CEO out in the field all the time, guarding a horse? Why wasn't he in the Peachtree Center, in an office with a large reception area, shmoozing clients and serving on crime advisory councils, and having lunch at the Ritz-Carlton downtown with the commander of the GBI?

I declined a second martini, ate my lobster tail, paid my tab, and went out to my car. It was twenty to seven. I headed back to Bella's Business Services and parked behind the building just after seven. Her back door would be three down from the left end of the mall. I got out of my car, got a toolbox out of the back, and went to the door. It was locked with a spring bolt on the inside, but the frame had shrunk a little since it had been installed and there was a sliver of an opening. I put on some crime scene gloves, turned the knob and held it there with duct tape. Then I got out a putty knife and tried to spring the lock tongue back with no success. I put the putty knife back and got out a flat bar. There was no one in sight. I put the bent end of the flat bar into the crack at the door edge and pried the thing open. It made some noise as the spring bolt screws inside tore out of the door, but if anyone heard it they didn't care, and no one came running. I untaped the doorknob and picked up the toolbox and went in and closed the door behind me. The spring bolt was hanging by one remaining screw. I went to the file cabinet. It was still light outside, but inside it was too dark to read the labels on the files, so I got a small flashlight out of the toolbox and held it in my cupped hand and went through the files. Denise was an orderly person. The files were alphabetized, so I found Security South quickly.

There was no way to conceal the break-in. Denise would report that someone was there earlier looking for

Security South, and she would remember that the someone had talked with her about her alarm system. They'd
assume that someone to be the burglar, and they would,
of course, be right. She'd probably remember that the
someone had said he was a private detective, from
Boston, which wouldn't help the Atlanta cops much, at
least until they contacted Delroy, and even if that led
them to me, and Denise ID'd me, there was no way to
tie me to the crime. So there was no reason not to steal
the file. And there was some reason not to sit in the bur-
gled office and read it by flashlight.

I put the flat bar and the duct tape in my toolbox, put
the folder in flat on top of the tools, and closed the box.
I went out, closed the broken door behind me, put the
toolbox in my car, got in and drove away. No one paid
any attention to me. I went up Peachtree Road, to the
Phipps Plaza Mall, and parked in their garage across
from the Ritz-Carlton Buckhead, took the file folder out
of the back of my car, went up to the first level, and sat
on a bench to read it.

It wasn't much of a file. It contained a collection of
invoices that indicated that Three Fillies Stables had
paid Security South an annual amount of $250,000. The
slips went back five years. Each invoice was marked
paid, with a check number and date entered in a nice
hand. There was a deposit slip stapled to each receipt
that told me that the amount had been deposited to an
account in the Central Georgia Savings and Loan
branch in Buckhead. There were also some Visa credit
card receipts, each neatly annotated in the same nice female hand, "Paid, PC" and a date. As far as I could tell,

Delroy had put the whole Security South operation on his credit card. Uniforms, guns, flashlights, ammunition, walkie-talkies. And as far as I could figure, somebody else had paid the bills. Penny Clive?

I found a place with a coin-operated copier and made copies of everything, put the originals back in their folder, drove back through the lively Buckhead traffic to the strip mall on East Paces Ferry, parked in back again, put on gloves again, went into Bella's Business Services again, and put the file folder back where it belonged. Then I departed. Scot-free. Again.

THIRTY-SIX

I GOT UP early, before the heat clamped down, and ran five miles through Lamarr under the wide-leaved trees. Back at the motel, showered, shaved, and happy with my breakfast, I got a cup of coffee to go and went to my room and sat on the bed and began to work the phones.

My first call was to the homicide commander of the Boston Police, my longtime friend and admirer, Martin Quirk.

"What the fuck do you want now?" Quirk said when they put me through to him.

"I've been away," I said. "I wanted to call and say hi."

"Oh Christ," Quirk said. "The best thing we ever did was fire you."

"You didn't fire me," I said. "I got fired from the Middlesex County DA's Office."

"We in the larger sense," Quirk said. "We in law enforcement."

"Jeez, since you made captain, you've lost a lot of that fun-loving warmth."

"Whaddya want?" Quirk sounded tired.

"I'd like any information you can get me on a former FBI agent named Jon Delroy. He spells it J-o-n. Before he was with the Bureau he was in the Marine Corps. Currently he runs an outfit in Atlanta called Security South."

"And why should I do this?"

"Because if I do it they won't tell me anything."

"Like they'll tell me," Quirk said.

"You're a captain. They'll pay attention to you."

"Sure they will—city police captains really matter to the Feds."

"Well, they matter to me," I said.

"Where you calling from?"

"Lamarr, Georgia."

"Good for you," Quirk said.

I gave him the phone number and he hung up. It was Tuesday. Susan gave a seminar on Tuesdays from nine A.M. to eleven A.M. It was nine-fifteen A.M. I drank my coffee and read the Atlanta paper until ten after ten. Then I lay back on the bed and tried to empty my mind—see if an idea popped up into the void. Mostly I thought about Susan with her clothes off. This would solve nearly any problem I had, but it didn't do much for the case. At eleven-fifteen, I called her.

"I've been trying to empty my mind," I said.

"I thought you'd already done that," Susan said.

"And just when I think I've done it—there you are with your clothes off."

"How do I look?"

"Like you do," I said.

"I'll take that to mean stunning," Susan said. "Are you doing anything else down there besides thinking of me with my clothes off?"

"Sometimes I sleuth a little."

"And?"

"And I'm compiling the results."

"Does that mean you're getting nowhere?"

"It's not exactly nowhere. I'm learning things. But generally I don't know what the stuff that I'm learning means."

"Let me help you," she said.

"Thank you, Doctor. Are you dressed?"

"To the nines. What do you have?"

"You remember the names of all the players?" I said.

"Of course I do," Susan said.

"How could I forget. Penny Clive and her sisters won't talk to me. I'm not allowed in the house or the stables or anywhere they own anything. The ban is enforced by employees of Security South."

"Are they still guarding the horse too?"

"I assume so. I can't get close enough to the horse or anybody else to find out. Both Clive husbands, Pud and Cord, have been tossed. They are now living together in Pud's former love nest in the heart of downtown Lamarr."

"Isn't Cord the apparent pedophile?"

"Yeah. Out on his own he's like a lost lamb, and Pud, amazingly, has taken him under his wing."

"Didn't you just mix a metaphor?" Susan said.

"Badly. Both men feel that Penny is the one who

gave them the boot. They feel that she's in charge and they also speculate that she has an intimate relationship with Jon Delroy, who runs Security South."

"He runs it? Isn't that new information?"

"Yeah. Apparently he *is* Security South. And apparently his only client is the Clive family. Even some of Jon Delroy's credit card charges were paid by someone designated PC."

"Penny Clive?"

"Could be. The charges appeared to be Security South–related."

"How did you find that out?"

"Burglary."

"Always effective," Susan said. "Are you looking into Mr. Delroy?"

"Quirk's checking with the FBI for me."

"What about the sheriff person, Becker?"

"Sheriff's deputy," I said. "I think he's a good cop, and I think he's honest. But the Clives have a lot of clout, and I don't think he can go anywhere with this on his own."

"Is he still using you to do it for him?"

"As best he can," I said.

"They have that kind of clout even with the father dead?"

"I think it was the father's money that gave him the clout," I said. "Now *they've* got it."

"The three girls?"

"Yes, equally. I talked with the lawyer for the estate."

There was silence on the phone line. I knew she was thinking. She'd have a very slight wrinkle between her eyebrows. And she would seem to disappear into the thought process, so that if you spoke she might not hear you. It was amazing to watch and the result was often lovely. I imagined her thinking. Dressed to the nines.

"It's Delroy, isn't it?" she said.

"I don't know," I said. "Might be."

"But he's the wedge in."

"Yes."

"He's the one that doesn't make sense. How long has he worked for the Clives?"

"Maybe ten years, maybe longer."

"Did your burglary turn that up?"

"It's an estimate. He was there when Pud joined the family, and he'd been there awhile."

"So Penny was a young girl when he arrived."

"I guess so—she's about twenty-five now."

"Still a young girl," Susan said.

"Maybe."

"Maybe?"

"Even when her father was alive she was running the shop on a daily basis. She is very different than her sisters. She's a young girl, but she's a tough young girl."

"Do you think Pud and Cord are right, that it was she who forced them out?"

"The problems in their marriages didn't change. What changed was that Walter Clive died."

"And Penny took over."

"Un-huh."

"Why would she do that?"

"I don't have a Harvard Ph.D."

"And I do," Susan said.

"And neither of us knows why she did it."

"Or even for sure, if."

"I couldn't have put it better," I said.

"I know. What about the mother?"

"Sherry Lark?"

"Yes."

"Might it serve you to talk with her?"

"I don't know. She's not around. She's an airhead, and a faraway airhead at that. She lives in San Francisco."

"Might it serve you to go to San Francisco? Mothers are often good sources of information about their children. Even airhead mothers, of whom there is a formidable contingent."

"Even in Cambridge?" I said.

"Especially in Cambridge."

"If I go to San Francisco," I said, "might you join me?"

"I might."

"Open your golden gate, don't make a stranger wait . . ."

"Stop singing," Susan said. "You remember the case you had when you were home? Kate and Kevin?"

"And Valerie Hatch," I said. "And her kid Miranda and her mother's dog, Buttons."

"Stop showing off. That case reminds me a little of this one."

"Nobody down here, that I know of, has a dog named Buttons," I said.

"No, but the more you get into the case, the more things are not what they appear to be."

It was nothing I didn't know, but it was worth reminding me of. It is hard to go through life assuming that things are not as they appear to be. Yet in Susan's work, and in mine, that is the norm. It always helps to be reminded of it.

"As we discuss this," I said, "could you undress, and tell me about it garment by garment?"

"Absolutely not," Susan said.

"You are so inhibited," I said.

"And proud of it," Susan said.

We were quiet for a moment. Then Susan spoke again and her voice had the sort of lush shading it took on sometimes when she was playing.

"On the other hand," she said. "As we've just discussed. Things are not always as they appear to be."

"This bodes well for our rendezvous by the Bay," I said.

"It do," Susan said.

THIRTY-SEVEN

- -

.

SUSAN AND I got a room at the Ritz-Carlton on Stockton Street, at the corner of California Street, halfway up Nob Hill. She was in the room when I got there, having come in from Boston an hour and ten minutes earlier than I had from Atlanta. She had gotten her clothes all carefully hung up, with a space between each garment so that they wouldn't wrinkle. She had her makeup carefully arranged on every available surface in the bathroom. She was wearing one of the hotel-issue robes, which was vastly too big for her, and she smelled of good soap and high-end shampoo. The clothes she had worn on the flight were already hung up. But underclothes and panty hose and magazines and packing tissue were scattered around the room like confetti after a parade. Workout clothes and sneakers and white sweat socks were laid out carefully on the bed. Along with half a bagel, and two PowerBars.

I was not used to being away from her as much as I'd been lately, and when I got the door closed, I put my arms around her and closed my eyes and put my cheek against the top of her head and stood for a long time without speaking while my soul melted into her. I knew we weren't the same person. I knew that it was good that we weren't. I knew separateness made love possible. But there were moments, like this one, of crystalline stillness, when it felt as if we really could merge like two oceans at the bottom of the world.

"We're pretty glad to see each other," I said.

"We should not be away from each other this long."

"No."

"Do you still want phone sex?" Susan said.

"I think I'd prefer the real thing," I said. "Now that I'm here."

"The real thing is good," Susan said.

"Except there's no room for it," I said, "unless we go lie down in the hall."

"I'll make space," Susan said, "while you rinse off in the shower."

When I came out of the shower the bed was cleared off and turned down. From the minibar Susan had made me a tall scotch and soda, and poured herself half a glass of red wine.

I picked up my drink and had a pull. It was lovely, pale and cold.

"No bathrobe?" Susan said.

"They're always too small," I said. "I guess they want to discourage people my size."

"Well, I don't," Susan said, and took off the bathrobe.

We spent a long time reuniting, and finally when we were lying quietly on our backs together with my arm under her neck, I said, "I'm very encouraged."

"Yes," she said.

We were quiet again for a long time, listening to the music of the spheres, and the occasional sound of the cable cars going up and down California Street. Then I took my arm from under her neck and got up and made myself a new drink, and brought it and her wine back to the bed. Susan wriggled herself sufficiently upright on the stacked pillows to drink wine. I handed her the glass and sat beside her with my back against the headboard.

"Have we been here together since I was out here looking for you?" I said.

"Fifteen years ago?"

"Um-hmm."

"I'm sure we have."

I was pretty sure we hadn't, but what difference did it make?

"Hard times," I said.

"I don't think about those times," Susan said.

"Ever?"

"I treat it as something that never happened."

"But it did happen."

"Not to the people we are now," Susan said.

"Well," I said, "who am I to argue mental health with a shrink?"

"You are the shrink's honey bunny."

"That'll do," I said.

THIRTY-EIGHT

AT SEVEN-FIFTEEN THE next morning, we walked down Powell Street in the glow of the early light off the Bay, to meet Sherry Lark for breakfast in a restaurant that called itself Sears Fine Foods, a little up from Union Square. I loved Sears Fine Foods. Their name overrated their cuisine a little, but every time I was in San Francisco I tried to eat there because, in tone and food, it transported me to my childhood. I thought that all good restaurants were like Sears until I began eating out with Susan Silverman. By seven-thirty we were in a booth, with coffee, waiting for Sherry.

Susan put her sunglasses up on her head when we sat down. She had on a black short-sleeved blouse and white pants, and a little black choker necklace. Her throat was strong. Her arms were slim and strong. I knew her thighs to be firm. She sat beside me, leaving the opposite side for Sherry.

Hippies are not slaves to the clock. Sherry arrived at

eight-fifteen. We had already drunk two cups of coffee, and the waitress had begun to hover around us with the menus. Sherry's gray-blond hair was twisted into a single braid that hung to her waist. She wore a folded red bandana as a headband, and what looked like an ankle-length, tie-dyed T-shirt. It was unfortunately apparent that she was braless. I stood up as she approached the booth.

"Sherry Lark," I said. "Susan Silverman."

They said hello and Sherry slid into the booth across from us. I sat down.

"Thank you for coming," I said.

"If it's about my girls, I'm always there," Sherry said.

The waitress pounced on us with the menus. We were quiet while we looked. I ordered scrambled eggs with onions. Susan ordered a bagel, no butter, no cream cheese. Sherry ordered waffles. Susan was watching her with a pleasant expression, but I knew her well. The pleasant expression meant she was registering that Sherry had no makeup, no bra, no socks, remarking that Sherry was wearing a long T-shirt and sandals. Susan was already sensing how seriously Sherry took herself, and smiling inwardly. The waitress brought Sherry herbal tea, and freshened up Susan's coffee and mine.

I said to Sherry, "Odd things are going on in Lamarr."

"Lamarr is odd," she said. "Stifling to the spirit."

"How so?" I said.

"All that rampant machismo, all that rancorous capitalism."

"Of course," I said.

"You know that the two are really mirror images of each other," Sherry said.

"Machismo and capitalism," I said.

"Absolutely. You're a man, you probably don't understand it."

She turned to Susan. "But you do."

"Yes," Susan said. "Naturally. Money is power, and power is all men ever care about."

Sherry nodded, approving of Susan's intelligence. She put a hand out and patted Susan's forearm.

"And they don't even know it."

Susan looked at me and I could see something glinting in her eyes.

"Duh!" she said.

"Lucky I have you," I said.

"It certainly is," Susan said.

"When's the last time you talked to one of your daughters?" I said to Sherry.

"Well, of course I talked with all of them at the funeral," she said. "And I talked with Penny about two weeks afterwards."

"About what?" I said.

"We . . ."

The food came and we were silent while the waitress distributed it. Sherry got right to her waffles. When she stopped to breathe, I said, "We . . . ?"

"Excuse me?"

"You started to say what you and Penny spoke of two weeks after the funeral."

"Oh, yes. Well, can you believe it? Walter left me without a dime."

"No," I said.

Susan still had the glint in her eye as she broke off a small piece of bagel and popped it into her mouth.

"I told Penny that I thought that wasn't right. I made him a home, and gave him three lovely daughters. I felt I deserved better."

"And Penny?"

Sherry chomped some more of her waffles. I wondered if she'd had a good meal lately.

"Penny has always been cold," Sherry said.

"Really," I said.

"Like her father," Sherry said. "I'm the imaginative one. The artistic one. I'm the one whose soul has wings. Penny is very . . . earthbound. Since she was a small child. She has always known what she wanted and has always done what was necessary to get what she wanted."

"She's practical," Susan said.

"Oh, hideously," Sherry said. "So practical. So material. So . . . masculine."

Susan nodded thoughtfully. I knew Sherry was annoying Susan. But I was the only one who knew her well enough to tell.

"You get along with Penny?" I said.

"Of course—she's my daughter."

Susan blinked once. I knew this meant more than it seemed to.

"But she's not sympathetic to your needs in this case," I said.

"Oh God no," Sherry said. "Penny is not the sympathetic sort."

"How about the other girls?"

"Stonie and SueSue are much more like their mother."

"Sensitive, artistic, free-spirited?" I said.

"Exactly."

"Did you know that they have separated from their husbands?"

"Both of them?"

"Yes."

Sherry chewed her last bite of waffle for a time, and swallowed, and turned her attention to the herbal tea.

"Well," she said finally, "they weren't much as husbands go, either one of them."

"All three of your daughters seem to have withdrawn," I said. "They don't go out, and people are prevented from visiting."

"Solitude can be very healing," she said.

"You think it's grief?"

"Their father provided for them very well."

"Do you have any theories why both Stonie and Sue-Sue separated from their husbands at this time?"

"As I said, they weren't first-rate husbands."

"They never were," I said. "Why now?"

"Perhaps Walter's death."

"How so?"

"Well, now that Walter's gone, Penny is in charge."

"And?"

"And she's always been a puritan."

"You think she forced the separation?"

"Even as a little girl she was full of disapproval."

I nodded.

"I was supposed to clean and cook and sew dresses," Sherry said. "As if I could reshape my soul to her childish materialism."

"You think she could have forced her sisters to give up their husbands?"

"I don't think her sisters would have fought very hard," Sherry said.

She signaled the waitress, and ordered two Danish pastries.

"They didn't love their husbands?"

"They married to please their father," she said, and took a large bite from one of her Danish. "They married men their father approved of, men he could control."

"How come Penny hasn't married?"

"She's young. And frankly, I think she frightens men. Men like pliant women. I find men are often frightened of me."

"You're not pliant," I said.

"No. I am fiercely committed to beauty, to poetry, to painting, to a kind of spiritual commingling that often threatens men."

"If Susan weren't here, I'd be a little edgy," I said.

Sherry smiled at me.

"Irony is so masculine," she said. "Isn't it, Susan?"

"So," Susan said.

She still had half a bagel to go. Sherry polished off the rest of her second Danish.

"Is it possible that Dolly Hartman had an affair with your husband twenty-something years ago?"

"The whore? Certainly she's capable of it, but twenty years ago? No, Walter and I were very close at that time. The girls were small, Walter was not yet the big success he became. No, we were a happy little family then."

"Dolly claims that she did."

"Well, she didn't."

I saw nowhere to go with that.

"What do you know about Jon Delroy?" I said.

"Very little. Jon was on the business side of things. I never paid any attention to the business side of things."

"Do you know how long he worked for Three Fillies?"

"Oh, I don't know. He was there before I left."

"How long have you been gone?"

"Nine years."

"And what was his job?"

"God, I don't know," Sherry said. "He was always around with his storm troopers. So tight. So shiny. So controlled. So anal-retentive. So full of violence."

I looked at Susan. She was studying the row of people sitting at the counter across the room. "Are you still with the guitar player?" I said.

"I'm not with anyone," she said. "Freedom is best pursued alone."

The waitress came by and put the bill down on the table.

"Whenever you're ready," she said.

I had been ready since Sherry Lark sat down, but I'd come all the way to San Francisco to talk with her. I made a final stab.

"Do you have any thoughts on who might have killed Walter?"

"I don't think of death. It's very negative energy. I'm sorry, but I prefer to give my full energies to life."

I nodded. Susan was still studying the counter, though I thought I could see the corner of her mouth twitch. I picked up the bill and looked at it.

"Would it be rancorous capitalism if I paid this?" I said.

"We both know if you didn't you'd feel threatened," Sherry said.

I paid. We left.

THIRTY-NINE

–––––––––––––––––––––

"**Y**OUR INSECURITY WAS pathetically obvious," Susan said when we were alone walking up Powell Street. "The way you grabbed that check."

"I feared emasculation," I said.

"And had you waited for her to pick it up," Susan said, "we'd have grown old together sitting there in the booth."

"You have any thoughts?" I said.

"Based on an hour of observation?"

"This isn't a clinical situation," I said. "We have to make do."

"I have no thoughts," Susan said, "but I can give you some guesses."

"Guesses are good."

"Well, she's not as stupid as she seems. Brief hints of intelligence slip through the hippie mumbo jumbo."

"Not many," I said.

"No. I didn't say she was brilliant. And mostly she

recycles things she's heard. But it is not uncommon, for instance, for fathers to encourage their daughters to marry men against whom the fathers can compete successfully. She may have simply heard it said, but she understood it enough to apply it to her husband."

"If it's true," I said.

"I told you these are guesses."

"What else?" I said.

I was trying to breathe normally, as if the climb up Powell Street were easy. And I checked Susan closely. Her breathing seemed perfectly easy. Of course, I was carrying eighty or ninety pounds more than she was. And I'd been shot several times in my life. That takes its toll.

"She's full of anger."

"At?"

"At her husband, at men, at Penny, at a world where she is marginalized, and probably at the guitar player who dumped her."

"Can I believe what she says about Penny?"

"No way to know," Susan said. "Her anger may be accurate, and well founded, or it may be a feeling she needs to have for other reasons."

"Do you think she loves poetry and beauty and peace and flower power?"

"I think she hates being ordinary," Susan said.

"You think she loves her daughters?"

"She left them when the youngest was, how old?"

"Fifteen."

"And she moved to the other side of the continent and she sees them rarely."

"So if she does love them, it's not a compelling emotion."

"No."

"And the money she didn't inherit?"

"It would have helped her to be not ordinary."

"It will support her daughters," I said.

"One thing you can count on," Susan said, "and this is an observation, not a guess: Whatever it is, it's about Sherry."

"All of it," I said.

"Every last bit."

"I'm more confused than before I talked with her," I said.

"And you came all the way out here to do it."

"Well, you came out too."

"Every dark cloud," Susan said.

We reached California Street. Susan paused for a moment.

"I'm willing to give in first," she said.

"You need to rest a little?" I said.

"Yes."

"Thank God," I said.

We stood on the corner watching people get on and off the cable cars. We were in the heart of Nob Hill hotel chic. The Stanford Court was behind us, the Fairmont across the street. Up a little past the Stanford Court was the Mark Hopkins, where one could still get a drink at the Top of the Mark. In the distance, the Bay was everywhere, creating the ambient luminescence of an impressionist painting. It imparted a nearly romantic glow to litter in the streets and the frequent shabbiness of the buildings. Behind us, below Union Square and along Market Street, there were so many street people, and they were so intrusive, that I didn't want Susan to walk around alone. . . . Being Susan, of course, she walked around alone anyway, in the great light.

"What's confusing you most?" Susan said.

"There's so much conflicting testimony from so many unreliable witnesses."

To the right, down California Street a little ways, was Chinatown, with its pagoda'd entrance, everything a Chinatown should be. And way down, on the flat, was downtown, which was everything a downtown should be. Even when no cable cars were in sight, the hum of the cable in the street was a kind of white noise as we talked.

"And yet there are some things which seem clear when I listen to you talk about it."

"Like it's clear that I don't know what I'm doing?"

"Like everything changed after the father's death."

"Maybe it was naturally, so to speak, the way it is now, and he prevented it."

"Or maybe someone else has stepped into his place and reshaped it," Susan said. "Either way, he was the power and now he isn't. So who is?"

"A number of different people say Penny, and they say so in pretty much the same terms."

"As Sherry," Susan said.

"Yes."

"As an outside observer, let me suggest that there is one thing which hasn't changed."

"Suggest away," I said.

"The security company."

"Security South," I said. "Jon Delroy. You like him for it, don't you?"

"He was there when the father was alive. He is there now," Susan said.

"Pud suggested that Delroy and Penny were involved sexually."

"What do you think?"

"At the time I thought it was preposterous. She's adorable. I was kind of offended."

"And now?"

"Now . . . well, we only know what we know. Delroy's still there, and several people say that Penny has the power."

"Life is full of heartbreak," Susan said.

"Luckily I have a fallback position," I said.

"You certainly know how to turn a girl's head with your slick talk," Susan said.

"The truth of the matter is," I said, "you are my position. Everything else in life is fallback."

Susan smiled and bumped her head once against my shoulder.

"You okay to walk down to the hotel now, old fella?" she said.

"Wait a minute, you were the one wanted to tarry awhile."

"Pity," Susan said. "I took pity on you."

We began to walk downhill on California Street, toward Stockton.

"We don't have to leave until tomorrow. What would you like to do the rest of the day?"

"I don't know, what would you like to do?"

I smiled.

"Oh," Susan said. "That."

I smiled some more.

"Afterwards can we shop?"

"Sure," I said. "If you're not too tired."

"I'm never too tired to exercise my rancorous capitalism."

"Nor I to display my rampant machismo," I said.

"A match made in heaven," Susan said.

We turned right on Stockton Street and went into the hotel.

FORTY

SUSAN AND I had hugged for an extended period at San Francisco Airport, before she got on a plane to Boston and I flew off to Georgia. Now, looking for my car in the Atlanta airport, I imagined that I could still smell her perfume and maybe taste her lipstick. Missing her was a tangible experience. I was already homesick for her, and by the time I retrieved my car and drove down to Lamarr I was quite sad, for a man of my native ebullience. I sang a little to cheer myself up, but "I'll hurry home to you, Lamarr, Georgia" didn't have quite the right ring.

It was hot even at night, and by the time I walked from my car to the hotel, my shirt was soaked with sweat. I made a drink in my room, and sat on the bed and sipped it, and thought about Susan. I had another drink, and when it was done, I rinsed out the glass, put away the bottle, took a shower and went to bed, and lay awake for a long time. In the morning, after breakfast, I got a call from Martin Quirk.

"Jon Delroy," he said.

"Yes, sir."

"FBI has no record of him ever working for them."

"Ah hah," I said.

"Ah hah?"

"It's a detective expression," I said.

"Oh, no wonder I was confused," Quirk said. "Then I ran him past the Marine Corps. They have a Jonathan Delroy killed on Guadalcanal. They have Jon Delroy, a lance corporal, currently on active duty. They have a Jon Michael Delroy, discharged 1958."

"My guy's around forty," I said.

"That's all the Delroys they got," Quirk said.

"Ah hah, ah hah," I said.

"That's what I thought," Quirk said.

I hung up from Quirk and called Dr. Klein. The woman who answered said he would call me back. I said no, that doctors did not have a good track record on calling back promptly and I would prefer to stop by. She asked if it was an emergency. I said yes, but not a medical emergency. That confused her so deeply that I was transferred to the doctor's nurse. After a lot more give-and-go with the nurse, I got an agreement that he would see me after hospital rounds and before his first patient. But only for a moment. The doctor was very busy. She recommended I get there by ten.

I did. At eleven-fifteen Klein came out of his office and grinned at me, and jerked his thumb to come in.

"So, you got by the guardians," he said.

"Barely."

"They're very zealous."

"Me too," I said.

"What can I do for you?"

"Tell me when the results of Walter Clive's DNA tests came back," I said.

"That's all you want?"

"Yep."

"I could have told you that on the phone."

"And when would you have called me?"

"Certainly before the end of the month," Klein said. He pushed a button on his phone.

"Margie? Bring me Walter Clive's file, please," Klein said into the speakerphone. Then he looked at me and said, "I've been keeping it handy until I figured out how to resolve the questions about his DNA results."

"I'm going to help you with that," I said.

Margie came in with the folder. She looked at me with the same deep confusion she'd displayed on the phone and then went back to her post. Klein thumbed through the folder and stopped and looked at one of the papers in it.

"I got the test results on May twentieth," he said.

"How soon did you notify Clive?"

"Same day."

"Are you sure you're a real doctor?" I said.

"I called him at once," Klein said. "I remember it because it was so unusual."

"So he knew the results on the twentieth."

"Yes."

"He's the only one you told?"

"Yes."

"Could anyone else have known?"

"He could have told someone."

"But nobody at the lab or in your office?"

"No. He used a pseudonym. I've told you all this before."

"If the pseudonymous report was in his file, how hard would it be to figure out whose it was?"

"It wasn't in his file," Klein said. "I kept it, along with Dolly's results and Jason's, in a sealed envelope in my locked desk until long after he was dead."

"Do you remember when he died?"

"Couple months ago."

"He was killed on May twenty-second," I said.

Klein sat back in his chair. On the wall behind him was a framed color photo of three small boys grouped around a pretty woman in a big hat. Next to it was his medical degree.

"Jesus Christ!" Klein said.

FORTY-ONE

— — — — — — — — — — — — — — —

When I pulled back into the parking lot behind my motel, a smallish black man in a baseball cap got out of a smallish Toyota pickup truck and walked toward me.

"Mr. Spenser," he said. "Billy Rice, Hugger Mugger's groom."

"I remember," I said. "How is the old Hug?"

"Doing good," Billy said. He looked a little covert. "Can we talk in your room?"

"Sure," I said.

We went up the stairs and along the balcony to my room. Billy stayed inside me near the wall. The room was made up. The air-conditioning was on high, and it was cool. Billy looked somewhat less unhappy when we had the door closed behind us.

"You mind locking it?" he said.

I turned the dead bolt and put the chain on. The venetian blinds were open. I closed them.

"There," I said. "Privacy."

Billy nodded. He sat on the neatly made bed, near the foot, leaning a little forward, with his hands clasped before him and his forearms resting on his thighs.

"How'd you know I was here?" I said.

"Everybody knows you're here."

"Does everybody know why?"

"Everybody be wondering," he said.

I saw no reason to dispel the wonder.

"What can I do for you?" I said.

"I don't know who else to talk to 'bout this," Rice said.

I waited.

"I mean, I talked with Delroy and he told me to just do my job and not go worrying about stuff I had no business worrying about."

"Un-huh."

"But damn! Hugger is my job. It *is* my business to worry 'bout him."

"That's right," I said.

"I can't talk to Penny 'bout it. She knows about it and ain't done a thing."

"Un-huh."

"And nobody broken no law, or anything."

"So why are you worried?"

"They ain't guarding him," Rice said.

"Security South?"

"That's right. They around all the time, and they keeping people out of the stable office and away from Mr. Clive's house and like that. But nobody paying no attention to Hugger, except me."

"They used to guard him closer?" I said.

"Used to have somebody right beside his stall."

"Anybody say why they don't anymore?"

"No. Like I say, Delroy shooed me away when I said something to him."

"Must think he's no longer in danger," I said.

"Why they think that?" Rice said. "The horse shooter killed Mr. Clive trying to get to Hugger."

"Maybe," I said.

"What you mean, maybe?"

"Just that we haven't caught the killer. So we don't know anything for sure."

"I been sleeping in the stable with Hugger," Rice said.

"Family?" I said.

"Me? I got a daughter, ten years old, she's in New Orleans with my ex-wife."

"You got a gun?"

"Got a double-barreled ten-gauge from my brother."

"That will slow a progress," I said. "You know how to shoot it?"

"I've hunted some. Everybody grow up down here done some hunting."

"What's he hunt with a ten-gauge, pterodactyl?"

"Maybe burglars," Rice said.

"So what do you want me to do?" I said.

"I don't know. I'm worried about the horse. You seemed like somebody I could tell."

"There a number I can reach you?" I said.

"Just the stable office, they can come get me. Don't tell them it's you. You ain't allowed in there."

"Who says?"

"Penny, Delroy, they say nobody's supposed to talk to you or let you come near the place."

"But you're talking to me."

"I'm worried about Hugger."

"I think Hugger will be all right," I said.

"You know something?"

"Almost nothing," I said. "But I'm beginning to make some decent guesses."

"I'm going to keep on staying with him," Rice said. "Me and the ten-gauge."

"Okay," I said. "And I'll work on it from the other end."

"What other end?"

"I'm hoping to figure that out," I said.

FORTY-TWO

- - - - - - - - - - - - - - - -

I SAT WITH Becker in his office. The air-conditioning was on and the blades of a twenty-inch floor fan were spinning in the far corner. We were drinking Coca-Cola.

"Two days before Clive was murdered," I said, "he learned for certain that he was the father of Dolly Hartman's son, Jason."

"Learned how?" Becker said.

"DNA test results came back."

"Hundred percent?"

"Yes."

"So he's got another heir," Becker said.

He was rocked as far back as his chair would go, balanced with just the toe of his left foot. He had taken his gun off his belt and it lay in its holster on his desk.

"His will mentions only his three daughters."

"Suppose if he'd lived longer that would have changed?"

"The timing makes you wonder," I said.

"There's other timing makes you wonder," Becker said. "Kid's about what? Twenty-five?"

"Dolly says she had an affair with Clive early, and then disappeared until Sherry was gone."

"Slow and steady wins the race," Becker said. "You figure one of the daughters scragged the old man to keep him from changing his will?"

"Or all three," I said.

"Why not pop the kid, Jason?"

"Old man is readily available," I said. "And if he included the kid, before they knocked the kid off, then his estate would be in their lives."

"You like one daughter better than another?"

"Well, that's sort of sticky," I said. "I figure Stonie or SueSue would be willing to do it, but would have trouble implementing. I figure Penny could implement all right, but wouldn't be willing."

"How about our friend the serial horse shooter?"

"Billy Rice came and told me that there's no more security on the horse."

Becker frowned a little. It was the first expression I'd ever seen on his face.

"Rice is the groom?"

"Yes."

"Well," Becker said. "Been couple months now."

"I know, but it's a valuable horse, and there's still security on the stable area and on the house. But no one's paying any special attention to the horse. Except Billy, who's sleeping in the stable with a ten-gauge."

"Case a hippopotamus sneaks in there," Becker said.

Becker let his chair tip forward. When he could reach the holstered gun on his desk, he tapped it half around with his forefinger so that it lined up with the edge of his blotter.

"So it seems like they're not expecting anyone to try to shoot their horse," I said. "Why would that be?"

"Might be that the horse shooter is a Clive," Becker said.

"And the whole horse shooter thing was a diversion?" I said.

"Except it went on for quite a while before the DNA results came back."

"How about this?" I said. "The killer or killers find out ahead of time about the paternity thing. They know Clive is going to have DNA testing done. They put the serial horse shooting in place so that if it turns out wrong, and they have to kill him, it'll look like a by-product of the horse shooting."

"It would explain why no one seemed to care if the horses died or not," Becker said.

"Yes."

"Nice theory."

"It is, isn't it?"

"Pretty cold," Becker said.

"Very cold," I said.

"Can you prove it?"

"Sooner or later," I said.

"Where's Delroy fit into all of this?"

"I don't know. Pud Potter says that Delroy and Penny Clive are intimate."

"Penny?"

"That's Pud's story."

"Was he sober when he told it?"

"Yes. The other thing about Delroy is that he's a phony. He was never with the FBI. He was never in the Marine Corps. And I'm pretty sure that there isn't any big company that he works for. Security South is him, working out of a letter drop in Atlanta."

"Well, you're a detecting fool, ain't ya?"

"We never sleep," I said.

"On the other hand, so he's bullshitting his way to success," Becker said. "Don't make him unusual. He's got the proper accreditation from the state of Georgia."

"That would mean his prints are on file," I said.

"Sure."

"Maybe you could run them for us, find out what he was doing while he wasn't in the FBI or the Marine Corps."

Becker took a pull at his Coke.

"Yeah," he said. "I can do that."

"While you're doing that, I'm going to commit several covert acts of illegal entry," I said.

"Be good if we get something that will be useful to us in court," Becker said.

"On an illegal entry by a private dick who's not even licensed in Georgia?" I said.

"Be better if you didn't get caught," Becker said.

"Be good if you don't look too close at what I'm doing."

"Be good if nobody asks me to," Becker said.

"Eventually I'm going to find out what happened," I said.

"Be nice," Becker said.

FORTY-THREE

I HAD A drink with Rudy Vallone at a restaurant called the Paddock Tavern, downstairs from his office. There was a bar along the right-hand wall as you came in; other than that, the place was basically the kind of restaurant where you might go to get a cheeseburger or a club sandwich, or if you had a date you wanted to impress you could shoot the moon and order chicken pot pie, or a spinach salad. There were Tiffany-style hanging lamps and dark oak booths opposite the bar, and a bunch of tables in the back where the room widened out. There was a big mirror behind the bar so you could look at yourself, or watch women. Or both.

"You're an industrious lad," Vallone was saying as he sipped a double bourbon on the rocks.

"Thank you for noticing," I said. "Did Walter Clive ever talk to you about changing his will?"

Vallone took a leather case from the inside pocket of his suit coat and took out a cigar. He offered me one. I declined. He trimmed the end of the cigar with some sort of small silver tool made for the task. Then he lit the cigar carefully, rolling it in the flame. Drew in some smoke, let it out, and sighed with contentment.

"Man, smell that tobacco," he said.

It smelled to me like there was a dump fire somewhere, but I didn't comment. Vallone sipped some more bourbon.

"Now," he said, "by God, this is the way to finish a workday."

"Did Walter Clive ever talk to you about changing his will?" I said.

"That might be considered a private matter between an attorney and his client."

"It doesn't have to be," I said. "Especially since the client got shot dead."

"There's something to that," Vallone said.

He puffed on his cigar and rolled it slightly in his mouth.

"And you've got some local support."

I cast my eyes down modestly.

"Dalton Becker has spoken to me about you."

"That is local support," I said.

"He asked me to be as helpful to you as possible. Said of course he wouldn't want me to violate any ethical standards, but that he'd be grateful for any support I could give you."

"Dalton and I have always been tight," I said. "Did Walter Clive ever talk to you about changing his will?"

Vallone twiddled with his cigar some more. He

seemed preoccupied with getting the ash exactly even all the way around.

"He talked about it with me once," Vallone said.

"When?"

"Before he died."

"How long before?"

"Well, you are a precise devil, aren't you. Maybe a month."

"What did he say?"

"Said he might want to change his will in a bit, would that be difficult? I said no, it would be easy. I said did he want me to get a start on drafting something up? He said no. Said he wasn't sure if he was going to. Said he'd let me know."

I drank a little from the draft beer I had ordered. "Did he ever let you know?"

Vallone took the cigar out of his mouth and shook his head. Had he left the cigar in his mouth when he shook his head, he would probably have suffered whiplash.

"Do you have any idea how he would have modified his will?"

"No."

"Or why?"

"None. Walter wasn't talkative. I think the only person he ever trusted was Penny."

"She say anything to you?"

"Penny?" Vallone smiled. "Sure—charming things, funny things, sweet things. Anything that gave you any information? Not ever."

"She understand the business?" I said.

"Recent years, she ran it. He was the front man mostly, since she got old enough. He'd shmooze the buyers, drink with the big money in the clubhouse, he and Dolly would take them to breakfast at the Reading Room in Saratoga. They could always get a table at Joe's Stone Crab in Miami. That sort of thing. Penny stayed home and ran the business."

"And the other girls?"

Vallone smiled.

"How'd they occupy themselves?" he said. "In the business?"

"Yes."

"They didn't. They had nothing to do with the business that I could ever see," Vallone said.

"So how'd they occupy themselves?" I said. "Besides boozing and bopping."

Vallone took out his cigar and smiled again. "They didn't," he said.

"So, boozing and bopping was all there was."

He nodded.

"Bopping and boozing," he said. "Boozing and bopping." He flicked his perfect ash into an ashtray on the bar.

"Well," I said, "there's worse ways to spend your time."

"And ain't that the by-God truth," Vallone said.

FORTY-FOUR

AFTER I LEFT Vallone, driving back to the motel, I noticed that I had picked up a tail. He wasn't very good at it. He'd get too close, then drop too far back, then have to drive too fast and pass too many cars so he wouldn't lose me. When we got to my motel I pulled into the lot and parked. He pulled in behind me, and went to the far corner of the lot, and just in case I hadn't noticed him, he turned the car around and backed into a slot where he could come out quickly if I took off. Pathetic. I sat in my car with the motor running and the a/c on high and thought for a minute or two. Then I got out and walked over to his car and rapped on the window. The window slid down and the cold air from the interior slipped out and wilted in the heat. The tail was a slim young guy with curly blond hair and aviator sunglasses. He was wearing a plaid summer-weight sport coat and he looked at me with an expression so studiously blank that it made me smile.

"Yeah?"

"Where's your boss?" I said.

"Excuse me?"

"Delroy," I said. "Where is he?"

"I don't know what you're talking about."

"The car's registered to Security South," I said, just as if I had checked.

"How you know that?" he said.

"It's why they make car phones," I said. "You picked me up outside the Paddock Tavern and followed me here. Worst tail job I've ever seen."

"Shit," the kid said, "I never done it before. You gonna tell Delroy?"

"Maybe not," I said. "My name is Spenser, what's yours?"

"Herb," he said. "Herb Simmons."

He stumbled a little over "Simmons" and I assumed it wasn't really his name.

"Why are you following me, Herb?"

"Delroy told me to. Said to keep track of you and make sure you didn't get near the house or the stables."

"The house being the Clives' house."

"Yes, sir."

"And if I did?"

"I was to call for backup and we was to apprehend you."

"Why?"

"Trespassing."

"Call a lot of backup," I said. "How long you been working for Security South?"

"A month."

"What'd you do before?"

"I was a campus police officer over in Athens. I never had to follow nobody."

"A good thing," I said. "Where's Delroy as we speak?"

"Up in Saratoga. Hugger Mugger's running in the Hopeful."

"So Penny's up there too."

"Miss Penny, everybody. Everybody goes to Saratoga in August. . . . Hell, I never been to Saratoga," he said. "Except when I was in the Air Force, I ain't never been out of Georgia."

"No reason to go," I said.

"You gonna tell Delroy?"

"No," I said. "How about your relief, when's he show up?"

"I got no relief. Delroy says we're shorthanded and I'm on you by myself."

"Hard to tail somebody by yourself," I said.

"Damn straight," Herb said.

"Why doesn't he cut back a couple of guards at the stable area, and help you out?"

"There ain't no guards on the stables no more. They figured it would be more efficient just to put somebody on you."

"Who do you call for backup?"

"There's guys at the house. I call them."

"Why are they guarding the house?"

"I don't know. I know nobody's supposed to go in there."

"Well," I said. "I'm going in now and have a sandwich, and watch the Braves game and go to bed."

Herb didn't know what to say about that, so he tried looking stalwart.

"Have a nice night," I said.

I walked back past my car and into the motel lobby. I looked at my watch. It was 6:35. I went through the lobby and out the side door and walked through the gas station next door and out onto the highway. It was about two miles from the motel to Three Fillies Stables. I strolled. Even in the early evening it was very hot, and by the time I got to the stable area at seven, my shirt was wet with perspiration. Mickey Blair was still there washing one of the horses with a hose. The horse seemed to like it. I could see why. It looked like I would like it.

"Hello," I said. "I'm back."

"Oh, hello," Mickey said. "I thought . . ."

"Yeah. I was let go, but now I've been hired again. Anyone in the office?"

"Nope. It's all locked up."

"Got a key?"

"Sure."

"I'll need to get in," I said.

"Why?"

The water sluiced softly over the small chestnut horse, who bent her neck a little so she could look around at me.

"Penny wants me to check something in the files."

"Nobody said anything to me," Mickey said.

"No, they wouldn't. It's supposed to be very hush-hush."

"Gee, I don't know."

"No, of course you don't and it's not fair to ask you," I said, "without explanation. Penny wants me to sort of check up on Security South."

"Security South?"

"Yes, Jon Delroy, specifically."

"She wants you to check up on Mr. Delroy?" There was something in Mickey's tone that suggested she thought it would be a good idea to check up on Delroy.

"She's afraid he's stealing from her."

"Damn!"

"This is the best time to do it," I said. "While they're all in Saratoga."

Mickey nodded. She could see that.

"So I figured I'd take the chance and tell you." I smiled at her. "Our secret?"

Mickey smiled. "Sure," she said. "Key's on a nail right inside the door to the tack room."

"Thank you."

FORTY-FIVE

THE FILES WERE locked, but I figured there'd be a key somewhere. People who would leave the office key hanging on a nail in the tack room wouldn't be terribly fastidious about the file cabinet. It wouldn't be too high because then Penny couldn't reach it easily. And it wouldn't be too far because people hate to bother. In about five minutes I found it, hanging on a hook in the lavatory, under a hand towel.

It took me a while longer to find anything interesting in the files. But it didn't take forever. The files were immaculately neat, which helped. Everything was precisely labeled, and everything was alphabetical, and near the back was a file folder with no label. I took it out. Inside were reports from Security South dating back more than ten years. There was information about Stonie at the truck stops, about Cord's problems with young boys, about SueSue's adulteries, and Pud's arrests for public drunkenness and assault. Each case included specifics of action taken and sums expended by Security South to resolve the problem. Most of these reports in the earlier years were initialed WC, and in recent years, increasingly, PC.

There was also a three-page typewritten report, unaddressed and unsigned, which in summary concluded that it was quite possible that Walter Clive had been having an affair with Dolly Hartman while he was married to Sherry, and it was entirely possible that Jason Hartman was Walter's son. There was a copy machine on the long table behind the desk. I ran the report through the copier, folded up the copy, stuck it in my back pocket, and put the original back in its folder. I assumed the report was by Delroy, and I assumed it was for Penny. There were no initials on this one, but there was no reason for Walter Clive to commission such research. He'd know whether he could have been Jason's father or not.

I spent about an hour more, but didn't find anything else to help me. It appeared from my fast glom of the files that Penny was running the business, and that the business was doing very well. I locked the files, put the key back, turned off the lights, locked the office door, and put the key back in the tack room.

Mickey had finished washing down the chestnut filly, who was back in her stall, looking out at me. Half a carrot would get me anything. Mickey sat on an upended plastic milk crate, reading *Cosmopolitan*.

"You got a carrot I can give her?" I said.

"In the bag," Mickey said, nodding at a black canvas backpack lying near her left foot.

There was a plastic bag of loose carrots in the pack, in among what appeared to be gym clothes and makeup. I selected one.

"Put it on the flat of your hand and let her lip it off," Mickey said. "That way she won't confuse your finger for a carrot."

"Hey," I said. "I was born in Laramie, Wyoming. You think I don't know horses?"

"Really? How old were you when you left?"

"Ten or twelve," I said.

Mickey smiled.

"Hold your hand flat, let her lip the carrot," she said.

Which I did. The chestnut filly took the carrot as predicted, leaving my fingers intact.

"You find anything?" Mickey said.

"Nothing special," I said. "What do you think about Delroy?"

"He works for my boss," Mickey said.

"I know that. But I figure anyone willing to exercise Jimbo has to have a certain amount of independence."

Mickey smiled at me. She had a wide mouth. Her big eyes were steady.

"Delroy is a creep," Mickey said. "He gives me the whim-whams every time I have to talk to him."

"Really? That's the way I feel about Jimbo."

"Jimbo's up-front," Mickey said. "He wants to kill you and will if you'll let him. Delroy's a slimeball."

"Don't beat around the bush," I said.

Mickey smiled. "You asked me," she said.

"What makes him so slimy?"

"He's so buttoned up and spit-shined and polite.

Kind of guy wears a blue suit to a beach party. But inside you know he likes to download kiddie porn from the Internet."

"Literally?" I said.

"Hell, I don't know. I just know he's not the way he seems."

"How?"

She smiled at me.

"Female intuition," she said.

"But Penny likes him."

"You bet," Mickey said.

" 'Likes' is too weak?"

Mickey shrugged.

"I don't know. Sometimes I think they're doing the nasty. Sometimes I think she just uses him for her purposes."

"Could be both."

Mickey shivered.

"God, how revolting. Being in bed with him. Yuck!"

"He ever make a pass at you?"

"Not really," she said. "He's too stiff and creepy. But he's a starer. You know? Sometimes when you first teach a horse to be ridden, you lay across the saddle on your stomach while he gets used to your weight. Which means your butt is sticking up in the air. If Delroy's around he's staring."

It had gotten dark as we talked. We stood in the small splash of light from the stable while around us the Georgia night, not yet black, turned cobalt. I took a card from my shirt pocket and gave it to Mickey.

"If you think of anything useful about Delroy, or

anything else, I'm at the Holiday Inn for the nonce," I said.

"The what?"

"Nonce. But you can always leave a message on my answering machine in Boston."

"I'd just as soon our conversation was private," Mickey said.

"Me too," I said. "Mum's the word."

"Not nonce?"

"Mum," I said.

"You talk really funny," Mickey said.

"It's a gift," I said.

FORTY-SIX

WHEN I GOT back to the motel Herb's car was gone.

The next morning, when I came down for breakfast, Becker was sitting in the lobby, reading the paper, with his legs stretched out, so that people had to swing wide when they walked past him.

"Morning," Becker said.

"Morning."

I walked to the door of the lobby. Across the parking lot I could see Herb's car. My personal tail. On the job. I turned back to Becker.

"Breakfast?" I said.

"Had some, but I can have some more," Becker said. "I like breakfast."

We went into the dining room and sat in a booth.

"Fella outside sitting in his car with the motor running," Becker said. "Know about him?"

"Yeah. He's been assigned by Security South to follow me."

"And by luck you happened to spot him," Becker said.

"They could have tailed me with a walrus," I said, "and been better off."

The waitress brought juice and coffee. We ordered breakfast.

"You know why he's tailing you?"

"He's supposed to make sure I don't go near Three Fillies—house or stables."

"And if you do?"

"He calls for backup and they restrain me."

Becker made a little grunt that was probably his version of a laugh.

"Be my guess that you don't restrain all that easy," he said.

"Maybe it won't come to that," I said. "So far, I've been outthinking them."

Becker added some cream to his coffee, and four sugars, and stirred it carefully.

"Got some stuff back on Delroy," Becker said. "He's got a record."

"Good."

"He used to be a cop. Then he wasn't. After he wasn't he was busted twice for scamming money from women. Once in Dayton. Once in Cincinnati. Did no time—in both cases the women changed their minds at the last minute and wouldn't testify against him."

" 'Cause they still loved him?"

"Don't know," Becker said. "But here's a clue. He served three years for assault in Pennsylvania."

"Think he might have threatened the witnesses?"

"Been done," Becker said.

"It has," I said. "Where was he a cop?"

"Dayton. I called the chief up there. Chief says Delroy was shaking down prostitutes. There was a police pay raise being debated by the city council. So they let him resign quietly. Which he did."

"They get the pay raise?"

Becker drank some coffee and put the cup down and smiled.

"No."

"Bet they're glad they let him walk," I said.

"They are," Becker said. "We don't like to go public on bad cops."

"Sure," I said. "Who'd he assault?"

"Don't know," Becker said. "Probably some nosy Yankee private eye trying to get the goods on him."

"Anyone would," I said. "You know what I'd like to see?"

"I've always wondered," Becker said.

The waitress brought our breakfast. Becker really did like breakfast—he had eggs and bacon and pancakes and a side of home fries. I had a couple of biscuits.

"I'd like to see Clive's last will and testament."

"Thought you talked to Vallone."

"I did. But I don't think Vallone says everything he knows all the time. In fact, call me crazy, but I don't think Vallone tells the truth all the time."

"And him an officer of the court," Becker said.

"What it looks like is that somebody in his family killed Clive to keep him from changing his will to include his illegitimate son."

After some work, I got a little grape jelly out of one of those little foil-covered containers and put it on my biscuit. Becker signaled the waitress for more coffee.

"They'd kill him to keep somebody from getting a quarter of what they were going to split three ways? Unless there was a lot less than we think, that doesn't make a lot of sense."

"It doesn't seem to. But what else makes any sense? He was killed two days after his DNA test confirmed Jason. Is that a coincidence?"

"Could be a coincidence," Becker said.

"And it could be a coincidence that the horse shooting stopped when Clive died."

"Or the shooter figured there was too much heat and went on vacation," Becker said.

"Sure, and the whole thing about the horse shootings and Clive being shot is just another coincidence."

"Or Clive caught the horse shooter in the act and got shot instead," Becker said.

"Which happened two days after he found out about his son?"

"It had to happen on some day," Becker said.

"Well, aren't you helpful," I said.

"I like your theory," Becker said. "But you know and I know that's all it is, a theory. You can't arrest anybody on it, and if you could, their defense lawyer would chew up our prosecutor and spit him into the street."

"Well, yeah," I said.

"So you need some goddamned evidence," Becker said. "Something for the DA to hold up in court and wave at a jury and say look at this. You know? Evidence."

"That's why I want to see that will."

"I'll get you a copy," Becker said. "It'll give me something to do."

"Here's something else you can do," I said. "I want to go out to the Clive house and rattle the cages, and I'd rather they weren't expecting me."

"I'm pretty sure I spotted several violations of the motor vehicle code on that car that's tailing you."

"Kid's name is Herb. If I was a fox I'd want him to guard the chicken coop."

"I can keep him busy for a while," Becker said. "Be kind of fun, almost like being a cop. Maybe I'll bully him a little."

The waitress put the check on the table. I paid it.

"You think this can be construed as a bribe?" Becker said.

"Sure."

"You want a receipt?"

"It'll be our secret," I said.

FORTY-SEVEN

As I PULLED out of the hotel parking lot I could see Becker swaggering over to Herb's car, looking very much like one of those small-town southern sheriffs we fellow-traveling northerners learned to loathe during the civil rights sixties—except that he was black. I smiled at the image and then it disappeared from my rearview mirror and I was out on the highway alone in the Georgia morning, heading for town.

I found Pud and Cord eating a late breakfast together in the coffee shop downstairs from their apartment.

"I'm going out and talk to your wives," I said. "Either of you care to join me?"

"They won't let you in," Cord said.

"Security South?"

"Yes."

"I'm a little tired of Security South," I said. "I think I'll go in anyway."

Pud was wiping up his eggs with a piece of toast. He

stuffed the toast in his mouth and smiled while he chewed and swallowed. His complexion was more tanned than I remembered it. His eyes were clearer.

"You going in either way?" he said.

"Yep."

"Want company?"

"You want to see your wife?"

"Yep."

"You quit drinking?" I said.

"Pretty much," Pud said. "Got a job too. Limo driver."

"Okay with me," I said. "You care to join us, Cord?"

Cord shook his head. "I don't want trouble," he said.

"Okay."

"When will you be back, Pud?"

"In a while," Pud said. "You'll be all right."

"What if there's trouble and something happens? What if they come looking for me?"

"If you'd feel better," I said, "go down to the Bath House Bar and Grill and tell Tedy Sapp I sent you."

"I know Tedy."

"I know you do. When we're through we'll meet you there," I said.

"Is that place open this early?" Pud said.

"Yes," Cord said. "I'll see you there."

He left us while Pud finished his coffee, and walked out of the coffee shop, neat and trim and walking erectly, struggling in parlous times to keep his dignity.

"He's not a bad little guy," Pud said. "They were pretty rough with him when they threw us out. He's scared, and he's lonely, and he doesn't know what to do.

He's trying to be brave. I feel like his father."

"It could get a little quick out at the old homestead," I said. "If they don't want us to come in."

"Ah hell," Pud said. "I'm with you, tough guy."

As I had when I'd first come there and met Penny, I parked on the street, and we walked up the long curving drive with sprinkler mist on either side of us. It was hotter this time and the air was perfectly still, the stillness made deeper by the faint sound of the sprinkler system and the occasional odd sound that might have been grasshoppers calling for their mates. The sky was high and entirely blue, and at the far corner of the house I saw Dutch loafing along toward the backyard.

I felt like I had just wandered into a Johnny Mercer lyric. Beside me Pud was quiet. He looked tight around the eyes and mouth.

On the veranda, with his uniform shirt unbuttoned and his gun belt adjusted for comfort, a Security South guard was sitting in a rocking chair, tipped back, with one foot pushing against a pillar, rocking in brief intervals. While the boss was up in Saratoga, the subordinates apparently let down a little. He looked up when I came onto the veranda. He frowned. Maybe he had been thinking of things that he liked to think about, and I had interrupted him.

"How you doin'?" he said.

He was lean and hard-looking, his hair trimmed short. He looked like he might have been an FBI agent once. I doubted it. I suspected he'd been hired because he looked like he might have been an FBI agent once.

"The ladies of the house at home?" I said.

He let the rocker come forward and let the momentum bring him to his feet.

"Sorry, sir." He was a little slow with the "sir." "They aren't receiving visitors."

I walked toward the front door. Pud was about a half-step behind me.

"The ladies don't live," I said, "that wouldn't receive a couple of studs like us."

The guard had a microphone clipped to his epaulet, with a cord that ran to the radio on his belt. He pressed the talk button on the radio and spoke into the mike.

"Front porch, we got some trouble."

The guard had his hand on his gun as he stood in front of me.

"Nobody goes in," he said.

"First you get sloppy with the 'sir,' then you don't say it at all," I said, and hit him hard up under the sternum with my left hand. He gasped a little and fumbled the gun from his holster. I got hold of his wrist with my left hand and came around with a right hook and he went down, except for his right arm, which I had hold of. I half turned and twisted the gun out of his hand and let it fall with the rest of him. I stuck his gun in my jacket pocket, stepped over him, and tried the front door. It was locked. I backed away from it and kicked it hard at the level of the handle. The door rattled but held.

"Lemme," Pud said, and ran at the door, hitting it with his right shoulder. The door gave and Pud stumbled into the hall with me behind him. It took us both a minute to adjust to the interior dimness. All the curtains seemed to have been drawn. Outside I could hear footsteps running, and then someone said, "Jesus." Then I heard him on the radio.

"This is Brill," he said. "Shoney's down, and there's someone in the house."

Pud was moving through the house. "SueSue," he yelled.

I took out my gun and stepped out of the front door and onto the veranda. The second guard, whose name must have been Brill, was there with his gun out, bending over Shoney, who was lying on his side only moving a little. Brill looked up and saw my gun and our eyes met. His gun was hanging at his side. Mine was level with his forehead. I didn't say anything. Brill didn't say anything; then slowly, quite carefully, he put his gun on the ground and stood up and stepped away from it. I walked over and picked it up and put it in my other coat pocket.

"Hands on the pillar," I said, "then back away and spread your legs."

He did as I told him and I patted him down. I had his only gun. I went over and patted Shoney, who was in some sort of twilight state. He had no other weapon either.

"Okay, sit there," I said to Brill, "and wait for reinforcements. If a head appears in that door, I will shoot it."

Then I turned and went back inside. The house was entirely still, as humming with quiet as the dead summer day outside. I looked around, remembering the layout from my last time. It was still dark with all the shades drawn. Then I heard Pud at the top of the stairs.

"Spenser," he said, and his voice was oddly quiet. "Get up here."

I went up the stairs fast. We didn't have much time before the arrival of more Security South guards than I could punch. The upper floor was as dark and still and cool as the first floor. The only sound was Pud's breathing and the subliminal rush of the air-conditioning. Pud was standing stiffly at the head of the stairs. Down the dark corridor, in the far end, were two dim figures huddled together, ghostly in white clothes. I found a light switch on the wall and flipped it. Squinting in the sudden brightness, the two white figures at the end of the hall seemed to shrink in upon each other in the light.

"My God," Pud said. "SueSue."

It was SueSue, and with her was Stonie. They were both wearing white pajamas, and they had backed tight into the corner at the far end of the hallway. Their hair was cut short. They wore no makeup. The distinguishing golden tan of the Clive girls had faded and they looked nearly as pale as their pajamas.

Again Pud said, "SueSue."

And in a voice without inflection and barely above a whisper SueSue said, "Help us."

The confiscated guns were heavy in my pockets. I took them out.

"Ever shoot one of these?" I said to Pud.

"No."

"Okay, this isn't the time to learn," I said.

I put the guns on the floor. And drew my own.

"Take one hand of each woman," I said. "You in the middle. We're going out of here at a run. Anyone tries to stop us, I'll deal with it. You keep them moving toward the car."

"What's wrong with them?" Pud said.

"I don't know," I said. "Get hold of them, now."

Pud hesitated another couple of seconds, then took a big inhale and went forward to the two women. He got each of them by the hand. They were childlike, putting their hands out for him to hold. I went down the stairs ahead of them, Pud behind me with the sisters.

Shoney was back on his feet when we went out the front door. He and Brill were looking a little aimless and uncertain as we passed them. They had no guns, and I had mine, so they made no move to stop us. We ran straight across the lawn, through the sprinkler mist, to my car, the women stumbling a little in bare feet.

"Put them in the backseat and down out of sight."

I went around to the driver's side and was in with the motor running when Pud joined me in the front. The Clive girls were lying in the backseat, SueSue above Stonie. I went into gear and we squealed away from the curb and out onto the street. As we turned the first corner, two Security South cars went bucketing past us, their flashers on, riding to the rescue.

"Jesus H. Mahogany Christ," Pud said.

He was still winded from running the sisters to the car. Breathing hard, he looked back at the two girls, still clinging to each other as if to keep each other from slipping away.

"Can they sit up?" Pud said between breaths.

"Sure," I said.

"SueSue, you and Stonie sit up now," Pud said.

Silently they did as he told them.

"You do this kind of thing often?" Pud said.

His respiration was normalizing.

"Usually before breakfast," I said.

"Man!" Pud said.

We turned onto Main Street. There wasn't much traffic. We passed a young woman in blue sweatpants and a white halter top, walking a baby in a stroller. A golden retriever moseyed along beside them on a slack leash. Pud eyed her as we passed. The ghostly sisters sat bolt upright in the backseat, their shoulders touching, looking at nothing. Pud looked back. No sign of pursuit.

"We can't just ride around all day," Pud said.

"True."

"Where we going?" Pud said.

"To a gay bar."

FORTY-EIGHT

"**W**HAT THE FUCK am I running here," Tedy Sapp said when I sat down, "a family crisis center?"

"You're my closest friend in Georgia," I said.

We were at Sapp's table near the door. Pud was in the back room with Cord, and SueSue and Stonie.

"First, Cord Wyatt comes in here like an orphan in the storm and says you sent him. Then you show up with the rest of the fucking family. What do we do when Delroy finds out they're here?"

"Maybe he won't find out," I said.

"I'm a bouncer, not a fucking commando. Delroy's got twelve, fifteen people he can put in here with automatic weapons. What's wrong with the Clive girls?"

"I don't know for sure. They've apparently been prisoners in the house since their father died. I don't know why. They're either traumatized or drugged or both, and it's like talking to a couple of shy children."

"Nice haircuts," Sapp said.

"You homosexuals are so fashion-conscious," I said.

"Yeah. I wonder why they cut their hair that way?"

"Maybe it wasn't their idea," I said. "Or the white pajamas."

"So what do you want from me?"

"I want you to look out for them, Cord and Pud too, while I figure out what's going on."

"And how long do you expect that to take?" Sapp said.

"Given my track record," I said, "about twenty more years."

"Becker will work with you," Sapp said. "If you get him something he can take to court."

"That's my plan," I said.

"Glad to hear you got one. What are you going to do about Delroy?"

"I'm hoping to bust his chops," I said.

"You figure he's the one?" Sapp said.

"He's at least one of the ones," I said.

"Delroy's a jerk," Sapp said. "But he's a mean dangerous jerk."

"The perfect combination," I said.

Sapp reached under the table and came out with a Colt .45 semiautomatic pistol, and put it on the table.

"On the other hand," Sapp said, "you and me ain't a couple of éclairs either."

"A valid point," I said. "Can you sit on things here while I go up to Saratoga?"

"Saratoga?"

"Yep. I want to see Penny."

"So, I'll bunk all the Clive castoffs here," Sapp said.

"And feed and clothe them, and watch out for them, supply bath towels, and clean sheets, and shoot it out with Security South as needed. And you'll go up to Saratoga."

"Yeah."

"That's your plan?"

"You got a better one?"

"I don't need a better one," Sapp said. "I can just walk away from it."

"You going to?"

"No."

"Then what are we talking about?" I said.

"It was a grand day for me," Sapp said, "when you wandered in here."

"Shows I'm not homophobic."

"Too bad," Sapp said. "Can any of these people shoot?"

"You got a shotgun?" I said.

"Sure."

"Almost anyone can use a shotgun," I said.

"If they will."

"Ay, there's the rub."

FORTY-NINE

- - - - - - - - - - - - - - - - - - - -

THE BAD NEWS about Saratoga was that it's about a thousand miles from Atlanta and I was driving. The good news about Saratoga was that it isn't so far from Massachusetts, and with a fifty-mile detour I could stop in Boston and pick up Susan. Practicing psychotherapy in Cambridge is a license to steal, and Susan, after a good year, had bought herself a little silver Mercedes sport coupe with red and black leather interior and a hard top that went up and down at the push of a button.

"We'll take it to Saratoga," she said.

"That car fits me like the gloves fit O. J.," I said.

"I'll drive," she said.

"I'm not sure I want to get there that fast."

"It'll be fun. I can buy a big hat."

"That's mostly why we're going," I said. "What about Pearl?"

"I already called Lee Farrell," she said. "He'll come and stay with her."

Which is how we got to be zipping along the Mass Pike, well above the speed limit, toward New York State, with the top down and Susan's big hat stashed safely in the small trunk space that was left after the top folded into it. Periodically we changed lanes for no reason that I could see.

"Tell me everything about the case," she said. "Since San Francisco and the dreadful Sherry Lark."

Her dark thick hair moved in the wind, and occasionally she would brush it away as she drove. She wore iridescent Oakley wraparound sunglasses, and her profile was clear and beautiful.

"I feel like Nick and Nora Charles," I said.

"Of course, darling. Would you like to stop at the next Roy Rogers and have a martini?"

"Not without Asta," I said.

"She loves Lee Farrell," Susan said. "She'll be perfectly happy."

I told her about the case. She was a professional listener and was perfectly quiet as I talked.

"So what do you hope to do in Saratoga?" she said when I was through.

"What I always do. Blunder around, ask questions, get in people's way, be annoying."

"Make love with the girl of your dreams."

"That too," I said. "All the principals are here: Dolly, Jason, Penny, and Delroy."

"I wish it were Sherry Lark that did it," Susan said.

"Because you don't like her?"

"You bet," Susan said. "She's self-absorbed, stupid, dishonest with herself."

"Isn't that a little subjective?" I said.

"I'm not a shrink now, I'm your paramour and free to be as subjective as I like. Who do you wish it were?"

We had crept up very close to the rear end of a Cadillac which was creeping along at the speed limit. Susan seemed not to notice this, but love is trust and all I did was tense up a little.

"Sherry'd be nice," I said. "But I can't see what her motive would be."

"Too bad," Susan said.

She swung suddenly left and passed the Cadillac and swung back in. The Cadillac honked its horn.

"Oh fuck you," Susan said pleasantly.

"Beautifully put," I said.

"So who do you think?"

"Well, it pretty much narrows down to Penny or Delroy or both. I'm hoping for Delroy. He's got a record. Even better, he's got a record for scamming women. But I don't see how all this could go down without Penny's involvement."

"Maybe he has some sort of hold on her," Susan said.

"Or she on him," I said.

"I thought you were fond of her."

"I am. She's beautiful, charming, twenty-five, and smells of good soap and sunshine," I said. "But you may recall the words of a wise and randy shrink—things are not always as they appear to be."

We passed West Stockbridge, and crossed the state line at breakneck speed. Susan smiled at me.

"I'm not so wise," she said.

FIFTY

IT WAS A near-perfect summer day, seventy-six and
clear, when Susan and I found Penny and Jon Delroy in
the paddock at the track in Saratoga a few minutes before the seventh race. The paddock was grassy, and
ringed with people, a number of whom, I assumed,
owned shares in Hugger Mugger. Billy Rice was there
with Hugger, their heads close together, Rice talking
softly to the horse. Hale Martin was on the other side of
Hugger Mugger, and the jockey was there. His name
was Angel Díaz. Like all jockeys he was about the size
of a ham sandwich, except for his hands, which appeared to be those of a stonemason.

"Hello," I said.

Penny turned and smiled at me brilliantly. If the
smile was forced, she was good at forcing.

"My God, look who's here," she said.

"This is Susan Silverman," I said. "Penny Clive, Jon
Delroy."

Susan put out a hand. Penny shook it warmly. Jon Delroy, on the other side of Penny, nodded briefly.

"What are you doing here?" Penny said.

"I wanted to see Hugger Mugger run in the Hopeful."

"I didn't think you knew what the Hopeful was."

"Sometimes I know more than I seem to," I said.

"Well," Penny said, again with the fabulous smile, "that sounds ominous."

Behind us the crowd noise from the stands suggested that the seventh race was achieving climax.

"Hugger's going onto the track," Penny said, "in a minute."

"Next race?" I said.

"Yes."

"May we join you inside?" I said.

"Of course. Are you a racing fan, Susan?"

"A recent convert," Susan said.

In Susan's presence, Penny still looked great, but a little less great, and the force of her charm seemed somehow thinner. Even the fabulous smile was maybe a bit less fabulous. The crowd noise quieted inside the track and we could hear the loudspeaker indistinctly announcing winners. With a boost from Hale Martin, Díaz was up on Hugger's back settled into the ridiculously small saddle, with his feet in the absurdly high stirrups. Hale nodded at Billy Rice, who, his head still next to Hugger's, began to lead the horse toward the track. The track police cleared a way. The horse seemed entirely calm, as if he were giving a ride to a kid at a picnic. Díaz did this every day, and looked it, calm bordering on boredom. He'd already done it several times today.

Hugger went in under the stands, heading for the track, and we followed Penny to her box in the clubhouse. Below us, and close, as befitted the owner of Three Fillies Stables, the dun-colored track circled the green infield. The big black tote board with its bright numbers looked oddly out of place. It wasn't, of course. It was the heart of the enterprise. It kept score. To our left the horses for the eighth race trailed down the track toward the starting gate. The eighth race at Saratoga was called the Hopeful. It was a race for two-year-olds. Of which Hugger Mugger was one.

I looked over the stands. This was an old-money racing crowd, by and large. The kind of people who kept a mansion in Saratoga to use in August, for whom that month's social life was devoted to horses. The town itself had a college and race month, a bunch of hand melons, some springs someplace, and twenty-five thousand year-round residents. Up higher from the track, as befitted her status as former concubine, I saw Dolly Hartman in a white dress looking at the track through binoculars.

I have never been much of a racing fan. It is two minutes of excitement followed by twenty-five minutes of milling. A full day at the track will produce about sixteen minutes of actual racing. I understood why. People had to get their bets down. That's why the horses ran, so people could bet on them. But since I got no thrill out of betting, the twenty-five-minute mill was boring.

On the other hand, I was there with the girl of my dreams, who was wearing a hat with a wide brim, exactly right for watching a horse race. Most of the other women wore hats, but none did so with Susan's panache. At the starting gate, one of the horses balked at going into his slot, and it took several people pulling, shoving, and almost certainly swearing to get him in there. The ruckus made another one buck in the gate and the jockey had to hold him hard, calming him as he did so.

A couple of guys in blue blazers and tan pants slipped into the box and sat behind me and Susan. I glanced back at them. They were young and intrepid-looking, with short hair and close shaves, and the look of bone-deep dumbness. Security South.

"How you guys doing?" I said.

Both of them gave me a hard look. One of them said, "Fine."

I gave them both a warm smile and looked back toward the track. Hugger Mugger was walking calmly into his slot in the starting gate. Susan leaned close to me and said, "Which one is Hugger Mugger?"

"Didn't you just see him outside?" I said.

"I was looking at the people," Susan said.

"Hugger's number four. Jockey's wearing pink and green."

"The one they just put into the thingy?"

"Starting gate, yes. One to the right of the one going in now."

The last horse was in the gate. There was a moment while they waited for everyone to settle down. All the horses were still. Then the gates popped open, the track announcer said, "They're off," and the horses surged out of the gate, as if a dam had burst. Around the first turn they began to stretch out. Hugger is running easily in

fifth place. Angel Díaz is hand-riding him. I look at
Penny to my left. She is bent forward slightly. Her knees
clamped together. Her mouth open. A hard shine in her
eyes. Her hands clasped in her lap. "Why doesn't he
hurry up?" Susan murmurs to me. Entering the stretch,
Hugger is still fifth. The four horses in front of him are
bunched. Accolade is on the rail. Bromfield Boy is
swinging wide on the outside. Reno is on Accolade's
right shoulder and Ricochet has drifted a little wider toward Bromfield Boy. All of a sudden a sliver of daylight
opens between Ricochet and Reno, and Angel Díaz puts
Hugger's nose into it as it starts to close. From where I
am, it looks as if his jockey turns Ricochet in toward the
rail to close out Hugger Mugger. The horses bump. Hugger staggers and bumps Reno on his left. Above the
banging of the horses, Angel Díaz bobs comfortably,
still with no whip showing. Hugger keeps his head
wedged into the small opening. He bulls into it with his
shoulders. His ears flat. His neck straight out. His head
swinging back and forth. He churns into the hole,
jostling Ricochet on his left and Reno on his right. He
keeps his feet, keeps his twenty-foot stride, with Angel
Díaz crouched over his neck, both of them buffeted by
more than a ton of full-gallop horse. Still no whip. And
then he is through the hole, his feet under him, and in the
lead. He is widening the lead as he crosses the finish,
looking as if he'd be perfectly happy to run that way
back to Lamarr if anyone asked him to. Everyone is
cheering, except of course for the Security South hard
guys sitting behind me. They only cheered at executions.

"My God," Susan said.

"Pretty good horse," I said.

Penny was on her feet, Delroy behind her.

"Where to?" I said.

She flashed me the not quite as fabulous smile.

"Winner's Circle," she said.

"Congratulations," I said. "We need to talk."

"I can't now. Tomorrow, breakfast at the Reading Room, eight o'clock."

"See you there."

"Your girlfriend's beautiful," she said.

"Yes, she is," I said.

And with Delroy right behind her, she headed off through the throng of people, some still cheering, many heading to the windows to cash in.

FIFTY-ONE

THE READING ROOM is actually a house, a large white Victorian next to the track, with a wide veranda where people can eat and look disdainfully out over the hedge at people who, not being members, cannot come in. I wasn't a member, but apparently Penny Clive was, and the mention of her name was entirely sufficient to compensate.

I was alone. Susan had decided to sleep in until nearly seven, and run before she ate breakfast. It was a decision she made nearly every day. I didn't mind. I never went to work with her either. I was the first to arrive. I noticed that there was only one other place set when they seated me on the veranda. A black waiter in a white coat poured me fresh orange juice, and a cup of coffee, and departed. I looked disdainfully over the hedge at the people going by. Penny arrived after I had finished the juice and half the coffee. I stood. But I wasn't quick enough to get her chair. The maître d' had it out and slid it gracefully in under her as she sat. Penny smiled at me across the table.

"Good morning," she said.

Undimmed by Susan's presence, Penny was in full luster. She wore a dress with a floral print of blue, white, and red. Her wide-brimmed straw hat was red with a blue band.

"You must have the hand melon," Penny said. "It's a local legend. The melons ripen every August while the track is in session."

"Sure," I said.

The waiter brought us two hand melons. They looked remarkably like cantaloupes.

"Wasn't that something yesterday," Penny said to me.

"Hell of a horse," I said.

"Angel rode him perfectly too."

"Do you know that Dolly has hired me to look into the death of your father?"

"Yes."

"Do you know why?"

"Yes."

"How do you feel about it?" I said.

I had, after all, ridden all the way out here alone with a shrink.

"I am very disappointed."

"Because?"

"I like Dolly, but she is exploiting our tragedy for her own benefit."

"By investigating your father's death?"

"By claiming her son as an heir."

"You reject that?"

"Entirely."

I ate some hand melon. It tasted very much like cantaloupe.

"Do you know where your sisters are?"

"They preferred not to come to Saratoga this year. This is really a business trip and they really aren't very interested in the business. All of us find the social whirl a bit too much."

"Yeah, me too," I said. "Did anyone tell you they've left the house in Lamarr?"

"Left the house?"

Either she was very good, or she really didn't know.

"Un-huh."

"You mean moved out?"

"Yep."

"Why? Where did they go? Are they all right?"

"They're fine. I think you need to talk with Delroy. He may not be keeping you fully informed."

"I . . ." She stopped and closed her mouth and sucked her lips in for a moment.

"I'll ask him," she said.

We finished our hand melons, and the waiter whisked them away and another waiter put down a corn muffin for me, and a soft-boiled egg with whole wheat toast for Penny. The egg was in a little egg cup and accompanied by a little spoon. I gestured for more coffee and got it immediately. I added some milk and sugar and had a sip and sat back. I wasn't even sure quite what I was trying to do, talking with Penny. And I didn't really know quite how to go about whatever it was I was trying to do. It wasn't a new feeling. I spent half my professional life in

that situation. Actually, I spent a good portion of my un-
professional life in that situation too. When all else fails,
I thought, try the truth.

"Ever since I came back into the case," I said, "I've
been stonewalled. Security South won't let me near you
or your sisters. I finally insisted a few days ago on seeing your sisters and I found them husbandless, apparent
prisoners in their own house, oddly disoriented. I took
them out and placed them with their husbands at a loca-
tion known to me and not known to Security South."

Something stirred behind Penny's face that made me
pretty sure she hadn't been told. It was only a little
something. She had great self-control.

"You had no right to do that," she said.

"Could you explain why they were being held as they
were?"

"They were not being held, Mr. Spenser. They were
being protected."

"From what?"

She shook her head slowly.

"I don't have to talk to you."

She was right, but I didn't think supporting her opin-
ion would do me any good. Having nothing to say, I
stayed quiet and waited.

"I love my family," Penny said. "I loved my father especially. His death has been a tragedy for me. I have
tried to protect us all from its impact. From the sometimes gratuitous scrutiny that follows upon a death. I am
still trying to protect us from that."

"Do you want his murderer caught?"

"In the abstract, yes. But I feel that Jon and the police

are adequate to that task, and what I want more than anything is peace—for me, for my sisters."

"Did you have anything to do with the separation of your sisters and their husbands?"

Penny stared at me. Her face showed nothing. She seemed to be thinking of something else.

"Do you have a relationship with Jon Delroy?" I said.

Penny looked tired. She shook her head again. Even more slowly than she had before.

"I find it hard not to like you, Spenser. But . . . I'm afraid this conversation is over."

She stood. The waiter leapt to hold her chair. She walked off the veranda and out of the Reading Room without another word and without looking back at me. On the assumption that offering to pay, as a nonmember, would be a vile breach of etiquette, I stood after she had disappeared and walked out as well.

FIFTY-TWO

WE WERE GETTING ready to go to a party at Dolly Hartman's house. Getting ready meant something different to Susan than it did to me. It began with taking a shower, but it did not end there. The shower was under way now. The wait would be a long one. While I was waiting, I called my answering machine from the Ramada Inn. There was a message to call Dalton Becker. Which I did.

"Got hold of that will you was interested in," Becker said.

"Wow," I said. "You never rest, do you?"

"Ever vigilant," Becker said. "Will was drawn up thirty years ago, right after Stonie was born, near as I can figure."

"And?"

"And nothing. Will says that his estate will be divided equally among his heirs."

"So why you calling me?"

"I miss you."

"You're being cute," I said. "Isn't that fun."

"And I got Vallone to talk to me a little."

"About something besides Vallone?" I said.

"Yeah, Rudy's always been pretty happy being Rudy," Becker said. "But while he was enjoying that, he did mention that Clive had discussed modifying the will."

I waited.

"You interested in how?" Becker said.

"Yes, I am," I said, "if you could get through swallowing the canary long enough to tell me."

"It pains me to say this," Becker said, "but Walter appears to have been a closet sexist after all these years. He wanted the will to add a clause giving managing control of Three Fillies Stables to any male issue."

"Jason Hartman," I said.

"That's the only male issue we know about."

"Why the hell didn't Vallone tell us that?"

"Maybe he forgot," Becker said.

"You believe that?"

"Rudy's pretty lazy," Becker said. "But he's made a good living around here for the last thirty years. And he's probably noticed that if he runs his mouth a lot about nothing, and keeps it shut about anything that matters, things work out for him. Especially if it matters to the Clives."

"Well," I said. "Now we've got a motive. If Penny knew the contents of that will and knew her father was about to change it and knew her father was going to acknowledge a son . . ."

"That's a lot of ifs," Becker said.

"Maybe I can make them less iffy," I said.

"If Penny was capable of murder," Becker said.

"She's capable of Delroy," I said.

"Good point. I wouldn't have believed that either if we didn't have to see it every time we looked."

The bathroom door was open. From where I sat I could see Susan get out of the shower with a towel. She saw me looking at her and smiled and flipped the towel like a fan dancer. I grinned. She grinned. Male issue might be overrated.

"You do anything with Herb the tracker?"

Becker laughed.

"Kid couldn't track a bull through a china shop," Becker said. "I sent him straight over to Hector Tobin's repair shop to get his car in compliance. Last name ain't Simmons, by the way. It's Simpson."

"Clever alias," I said. "You talked to Tedy Sapp at all?"

"Nope. He's got no time for me. He's too busy looking after the brood of refugees you dumped on him."

"You know about that."

"I sort of pay attention. I got nothing much else to do."

"You ready to move on Penny?" I said.

" 'Cause you don't like her boyfriend? Or whatever he is."

"She's got opportunity, and motive."

"Un-huh."

"She's got Delroy."

"Un-huh," Becker said. "You got a murder weapon?"

"No."

"Eyewitness?"

"No."

"Fingerprints? Powder residue? Confession? Any of that kind of stuff?"

"If we can arrest somebody, and pressure somebody, we can turn somebody."

"Sure, do it all the time with guys rob a convenience store. But these aren't guys robbed a convenience store. These are Clives. Gimme some evidence."

"Maybe the sisters will be in shape to talk with me," I said.

"I'd like to hear what her sisters have to say."

"Okay. Everybody who is anybody is heading back down to Lamarr tomorrow. Me too. I'll talk to SueSue and Stonie this weekend."

"I'm looking forward to it," Becker said.

"Because you thirst for justice?"

"Because I always like to see what happens after somebody pokes a stick into a hornet's nest."

We hung up and I sat for a bit in my chair, thinking and looking at Susan. With the towel contrived in some way to cover all areas of special interest to me, Susan was sitting in the sink in the bathroom, applying her makeup. I wasn't startled by her position anymore. She liked a lot of light and she liked to get close to the mirror and she was small enough so she could, and she took a long time putting on her makeup, so she sat in the sink. Once I'd asked her about it and she had turned the question back. "Wouldn't you sit in the sink," she had said, "if you weren't so big and didn't fit?"

I was now at a point where I didn't understand why anyone wouldn't sit in the sink.

DOLLY HARTMAN'S COTTAGE in Saratoga was a cottage in name only. It had Greek Revival columns out front, and a big dining room with a fifteen-foot ceiling where hors d'oeuvres were spread upon a lace table-cloth, and champagne chilled in silver buckets. A couple of kids who would have looked comfortable in jeans looked quite uncomfortable in French maid outfits as they circulated through the house pouring champagne. Dolly was there being the hostess with the mostess in a gauzy white gown that had several layers and made her look vaguely like Little Bo-Peep. Her son, Jason, was with her, greeting guests, looking polished in a crisp black shirt buttoned to the neck, and black linen trousers. Susan got a glass of champagne, which she used mainly as a prop, and went to the buffet table, which, she knew, was where the action would be. People interested Susan. She also knew I needed to be alone with Dolly.

"How are you doing?" Dolly said.

"I keep learning more and more, and knowing less and less," I said. "You're sure you can't think of anyone at all that knew of Walter's DNA testing?"

"Me, Walter, and Dr. Klein," Dolly said. "I can't believe Walter told anyone but me. He was very secretive. Dr. Klein didn't even tell me."

"Walter told you?"

"Yes. He called me—the night before he died, as a matter of fact—and told me. He was quite excited about it."

"Dr. Klein have a relationship with anyone in the Clive family?" I said.

Dolly was silent for a moment, as if examining something she'd never seen before. Then she smiled.

"I do believe that Larry might have had a little fling with the Hippie."

"Sherry Lark?"

"Or whatever her name is this week," Dolly said.

"How recent a fling?"

Dolly smiled some more.

"Did you ever see the play *Same Time Next Year*?"

"I know the premise," I said.

"Well, it's like that, sort of, I think. Larry and the Hippie would gather occasionally, when she came to Lamarr to see her daughters, or when Larry went to San Francisco to a medical conference."

"He's married."

"Yes," Dolly said. "And happily, as far as I can tell. I think Sherry was his walk on the wild side, and God knows he would have been discreet about it."

"How do you know about it?" I said.

Dolly smiled widely, and there was a small flush on her lovely cheekbones. She didn't say anything. *Larry Klein, you dog.*

"Do you think they might still be, ah, relating?" I said.

"If they were, I assume they still are."

"Possibly. . . . Men sometimes reveal confidences to women with whom they are sleeping," I said.

"Really?" Dolly said. "I'm shocked. Shocked, I tell you."

I went to find Susan.

FIFTY-THREE

I GOT TO Lamarr with the taste of lipstick from Susan's goodbye kiss no longer lingering, but its memory still insistent. Back in my old digs at the Holiday Inn Lamarr, I unpacked my toothbrush and bullets, slept the night, and at seven the next morning was in the hospital cafeteria with Larry Klein, M.D.

"How are things going?" Klein said as he organized a couple of sausage biscuits on his plate.

"Curiouser and curiouser," I said. "Do you know Sherry Lark?"

Klein smiled.

"Since she was Sherry Clive," he said.

"Have you seen her recently?"

Klein shrugged, and bit into a biscuit.

"You ask a noncommittal question," I said, "you get a noncommittal answer. When's the last time you saw Sherry?"

"Wow, that sounds a little coppish," Klein said. "I thought we were pals."

"I am a little coppish," I said. "And there's a point at which I'm nobody's pal."

"This the point?"

"It's past the point. When did you see her last?"

"May, I think. She came to my office."

"And got right in?" I said.

"We're old friends."

"Social visit?"

"She thought she had a cold. She didn't. She had a seasonal allergy. I gave her some antihistamine samples I had."

"You mention Walter Clive?"

Klein stared at me. I could feel him starting to close down.

"I don't remember. I might have. He's a friend, she's a friend, they used to be married."

I drank some more coffee.

"Here's the thing," I said. "I think Walter Clive was killed because of his DNA tests. I think someone knew he was having them and started the horse shooting as a cover-up pending the outcome of the tests."

"Jesus," Klein said.

"If the tests were negative, the horse shootings would stop and everything would go on as before. If he did have a son, he got shot and the cops think it's the horse shooter."

"For God's sake, Spenser, who would be so . . . so . . . Who would plan something like that out?"

"Clive was planning to rewrite his will in favor of male issue, if any."

Klein looked suddenly as if he had bitten into a toad.

"Only you, Clive, and Dolly knew about Clive's blood testing," I said. "Only you and Clive knew the results. He told Dolly. Who did you tell?"

Klein's face had reddened as I talked, and then as I waited for his answer it began to drain, until it was pale and he looked as if he might fall over. If he did, he was in the right place. There'd be a good response to *Is there a doctor in the house*? I waited.

"I . . . I've known Sherry half her life," Klein said.

I drank some of my coffee. It wasn't very good coffee. But it was hot and contained caffeine, so it was sufficient.

"I can't believe . . ." Klein looked at his partly eaten sausage biscuit for a moment and then pushed it away. Good idea.

I waited. His face began to redden again. Good sign. He probably wasn't going to fall over.

"You know," he said without looking at me, "that in every elevator, in the washrooms, and in the medical locker rooms, there are these signs that read, 'Respect Patient Confidentiality.' "

"I've seen them," I said.

Klein shook his head slowly. "Jesus Christ," he said.

"You told her," I said. "Didn't you?"

"Yes."

"You were pretty good friends, and after all it did involve her ex-husband and, indirectly, her daughters, and what harm would it do? For crissake, she lived way out in San Francisco."

"Something like that."

"When did she first know?" I said.

"A little while after Walter arranged for the tests. I was in San Francisco, at an internal medicine conference. We had dinner together, some wine, you know."

"Un-huh. And when did she learn the results?"

"She came to Lamarr that week," Klein said.

"Amazing how things fall into place, isn't it."

"She stopped by my office, like I said."

"And?" I said.

"We talked about this and that for a while . . . and I guess it came up . . . and I told her."

"When?"

Klein closed his eyes as if thinking back over the scene.

"Walter's folder was still on my desk. I remember her seeing it, and commenting. It's probably what gave rise to the question."

"Sure," I said.

"You think she came on purpose, to find out?"

"Yes. Why was the folder out?"

"I had called Walter with the results."

"So she knew the same day he did."

"Yes."

My coffee cup was empty. I went up to get some more, and when I came back Klein had his head in his hands.

"Does anyone have to know this?"

"Probably not," I said. "I won't mention it if I don't have to."

"I never thought . . . You think it led to the murder, don't you?"

"Yes."

"You think Sherry did it?"

"To protect her girls?" I said.

"Oh, I don't think so," Klein said. "She wasn't a dedicated mother."

"I gather. If so, then she had no motive."

"Hatred of Dolly?" Klein said.

I nodded slowly.

"That would be a motive," I said.

"Sherry is very odd," Klein said. "I . . ." He let it trail away.

I drank some more of the bad coffee.

"Tell me something," I said. "I don't mean to pry, but when you and she were having sex, did she whisper things like 'Right on' and 'Give peace a chance'?"

Klein's head jerked up and he stared at me with his mouth hanging open. He shut it and opened it again and said nothing and shut it.

"None of my business anyway," I said.

"How did you know we had sex?" Klein said hoarsely.

"I'm a detective," I said.

I WENT BACK to my motel, hoping that Dr. Klein didn't have a complicated diagnosis today. It was quarter to nine when I got there. I went to the dining room and had breakfast. In the middle of breakfast I had a thought. I was pleased to have it. I'd had so few recently.

Knowing that Walter was having paternity DNA test-ing was not enough information to get him killed. Someone would also have to know about the prospec-tive change in his will. I finished breakfast and went to see Rudy Vallone.

"Dalton Becker says that Clive was planning to change his will," I said when I was in his office and seated in front of his desk.

"Always right to the point," Vallone said.

"Always," I said. "Somebody had to know that be-sides Clive."

"Why?"

"Trust me," I said. "Who could have known Clive's intention besides you?"

"It was merely inquiry, sir. It was not yet an intention."

"Who knew of his inquiry?"

"Whoever he may have told," Vallone said.

"You didn't tell anyone?"

"Of course not."

I had another thought, two in the same morning. And this one was inspired.

"You know Sherry Lark?" I said. "The former Mrs. Clive?"

"Of course," Vallone said.

"You tell her?"

I thought Vallone colored a little bit. That's probably as close as lawyers can get to blushing.

"Of course not," Vallone said. "Why on earth would I tell Sherry?"

"In a fit of passion," I said.

Vallone colored a little more.

"Excuse me?"

"Listen," I said. "I can find this out. It's just time and money and I've got some of both. But why drag it out? Sherry's a free spirit. She probably had reason to want to prove herself desirable, and to do so with her husband's associates. You bopped her, didn't you?"

Vallone struggled for a moment but his essential self won out. He bragged about it. "Her idea," he said. He leaned back in his chair and took out a cigar and began to trim the end with a small silver knife.

"Last time she was in town she came to see me. I knew her from the old days. We, ah, used to get together now and then, and when she came to see me this time, she said she was hoping we could sort of pick up where we left off so long ago."

He paused while he got his cigar burning. "You've seen her?"

I nodded.

"Sherry's still a fine-looking woman to my eye, and . . ." He shrugged.

I waited.

"Right there on that couch," he said.

"And in those scant moments when you weren't telling each other how it was just like it always was, she might have asked about Walter and you might have let slip that he was thinking of changing his will."

"You know how it is when you're in heat," Vallone said.

"I'm proud to say that I do."

* * *

At TEN-THIRTY, WHICH would make it seven-thirty Pacific time, I called Sherry Lark. It was probably too early; my memory was that hippies slept late. But it was as long as I could stand to wait.

When she answered her voice told me I was right. She'd been asleep.

"Spenser," I said, "remember me? Square-jawed, clear-eyed, waffles at Sears?"

"Oh . . . yeah . . . sure. Why are you calling me?"

"For this case I'm working on," I said. "Did you tell all your daughters about Walter's DNA results, or just Penny?"

"Whaaat?"

"Come on, Sherry, I know you knew, and I know you told. I'm only asking which ones."

"I'm not about to betray my daughters . . ."

"I know a homicide cop out there named O'Gar," I said. "If I ask him to, he'll come and haul your flower child butt down to the Hall of Justice and question you in a back room under hot lights."

"I . . ."

"Who'd you tell, Sherry? It's either me, now, the easy way, or O'Gar, soon, the hard way."

"I only told Penny. She's the only one with the spunk to stand up to her father."

"And you told her he was planning to change his will."

"He was going to give their inheritance to that whore's bastard."

"And you couldn't tolerate her winning like that," I said.

"I'm looking out for my daughters," she said.

"Mother love," I said.

And hung up. I didn't think Sherry Lark had killed Walter Clive. But somebody had, and Penny kept looking better.

FIFTY-FOUR

I SAT WITH Tedy Sapp and the Clive outcasts around a big table eating pizza in the corner of the Bath House Bar and Grill. Sapp was drinking coffee. Everyone else had iced tea, except me. I didn't like iced tea. Sapp was beside me to my right. Cord Wyatt was on the other side. Beyond him was Stonie, then SueSue, then Pud. All of the Clive exiles were looking better than they had. Pud's eyes were clear and his face had lost a lot of the ruddy mottle that he used to sport. Cord seemed more at ease in these surroundings. The two women had brushed their short hair as best they could and put on makeup. They were dressed normally. Life had returned to their eyes. And their bearing was no longer feral.

Since she had once called me a hunk, I figured SueSue was the one I should talk to.

"Tell me what happened to you," I said.

Sitting beside SueSue, Pud put his open hand on her

back and patted a little. SueSue looked at Stonie. She took a deep breath through her nose.

"After Daddy . . . died, Penny sat down with us. She said that it was terrible that Daddy had died. But that we shouldn't worry, that she could run things, in fact she had run things for a while, and Three Fillies would go on as if Daddy were alive."

She stopped and looked at Stonie again.

"Go ahead," Stonie said. "Tell everything. We've been pretending much too long. Let's get everything out."

SueSue took in more air.

"Okay. Penny also said that both Stonie and I had to make some changes. She said Pud was a drunk and was sucking money out of the business and bringing nothing back."

"She got that right," Pud said.

He still had his open hand resting on her back.

"She said Cord . . ."

SueSue looked at Cord.

"She said Cord was a queer," Cord finished for her.

Stonie and Cord didn't touch, but they seemed comfortable beside each other. SueSue nodded.

"And she said we had to get rid of them," SueSue said. "They had to be purged from our family the way stuff sometimes has to be purged from a body."

"Poisonous," Cord said.

"Then she said we had to purge ourselves. She said the family was disgraced by us, drunks and whores, she said. She said that we were required to stop smoking and drinking and whoring. She said no more makeup, no fancy clothes, nothing. She said until we were clean we would need to sequester ourselves, like nuns or something—she had a fancy phrase, but I can't remember it exactly. We were not to leave the house."

"Did you object?" I said, just to keep her going.

"Sure, but Jon Delroy was there and his men were all around. Daddy was dead. I was afraid of her, afraid of them."

"You too?" I said to Stonie.

"Cord and I had been unhappy for a very long time," Stonie said. "It deadens you."

Cord patted her hand. She smiled at him.

"Not much fun for you either, was it?" she said.

Cord shook his head.

"So," SueSue said, "she had our hair cut short, like you see, and she took our clothes and had the windows closed up and we had to take some pills."

"Sedatives?" I said.

"I guess so. Things are a little foggy."

"They were full of something when they came here," Sapp said. "Took some time to get them back."

"You do that?"

"I had some help."

"I owe you," I said.

"You bet you do," Sapp said.

SueSue was impatient. She had a story to tell, and everyone was listening. She liked having everyone listening.

"No television, no radio, nothing to read," she said. "Like we had to clear our minds."

"How do you get on with your mother?" I said.

SueSue and Stonie looked at each other.

"My mother?" SueSue said.

"Sherry Lark?" Stonie said. There was a lot of distaste in the way she said "Lark."

"My mother's a dipshit," SueSue said.

"How did she get along with Penny?"

"Penny hated her."

"How'd Penny get along with your father?"

"She loved Daddy," SueSue said.

"We all loved Daddy," Stonie said.

"Do you mean more than you're saying?"

"Well." Stonie had a lot less effect than SueSue. "We did love Daddy, all three of us. But maybe we didn't love him the right way, and maybe we'd have been better if we'd loved him some other way."

"What the hell does that mean?" SueSue said.

"I don't know exactly how to say what I'm trying to say. But we all loved Daddy, and look at us."

"It's not Daddy's fault," SueSue said.

"What do you think about Jason Hartman?" I said.

It diverted them.

"Jason?" SueSue said. "What about Jason?"

"My question exactly."

"He's cute," SueSue said.

Stonie nodded.

"He's sort of like a relative," she said. "Being Dolly's son and all."

"Know anything unusual about him?"

"No," Stonie said. "Except he doesn't seem to do much. Doesn't work. Lives with his mother."

"Maybe he's in your program, Cord," Pud said.

"He is very cute," Cord said.

Stonie patted Cord's hand.

"Shhh," she said.

They both smiled.

"Why do you ask?" SueSue said.

It would have been great theater to say, *Because he's your brother*, but it didn't seem to get me anywhere.

"Do you know the terms of your father's will?" I said.

"We inherit everything, the three of us," SueSue said.

"But Penny runs things," Stonie said. "Neither one of us knows anything about business."

"She sharing equally?" I said.

"The estate hasn't been settled yet, but Penny gives us both money."

"How are you feeling about Penny?"

"I don't know," SueSue said. "I mean, she's our sister and she's taking care of us."

"And she locked us up and broke up our marriages," Stonie said.

"Our marriages were already broken," SueSue said. "Penny's always been bossy."

Sapp looked at me. I nodded.

"Now I know why the caged bird sings," I said.

"What the hell does that mean?" SueSue said.

"I don't know," I said. "It's too hard for me."

FIFTY-FIVE

THE CALL WOKE me early in the morning, just after sunrise.

"You want to know who killed Walter Clive," somebody whispered, "get on Route 20. Drive twenty miles west from the Lamarr exit. Park on the shoulder. Get out of the car and wait."

"What time?" I said.

"Be there at midnight tonight. Alone. We'll be able to see you for miles."

"How nice for you," I said.

The whisperer hung up. I tried dialing *69, but it didn't work on the motel extension. I looked at my watch. Quarter to six. I got up, showered, and went to my car. When I got onto Route 20 I set the trip clock on my car, and in twenty miles, I stopped. It was open country with gentle hills and some tree cover. The whisperer was right; they could see me coming. I went on to the next exit, turned around, and headed back to town.

Tedy Sapp was out of bed when I got to the Bath House Bar and Grill, drinking coffee in the empty bar with a slender gray-haired man in a light tan summer suit and a blue oxford shirt. There was a box of cinnamon donuts open on the table.

"Once a cop, always a cop," I said, and took a donut.

"This is Benjamin Crane," Sapp said. "My main squeeze."

We shook hands. He grinned at Tedy.

"Gotta go," Crane said. "You have business, and I have to gaze into many eyes."

He left.

"Been together long?" I said to Sapp.

"Ten years."

"Love's a good thing," I said.

"Even the one that dare not speak its name?"

"Even that one."

Sapp poured me a cup of coffee. I drank it and ate my donut while I told him the deal.

"Called early," Sapp said, "so they'd be sure to get you."

"Yep."

"It's a setup," Sapp said. "And a stupid one. They gave you all day to figure it out."

"The price they paid for calling early," I said. "I figure it's Delroy."

"Good choice," Sapp said. "He's stupid enough. You're going to need help with this."

"I know," I said. "You got a rifle?"

"Yep."

I had a street map of Columbia County I had bought

when I first arrived. Sapp and I studied it on the table.

"Here's about where they want you," Sapp said.

"I know," I said. "I've been out there."

"Of course you have," Sapp said. "It's not a bad spot for them. Used to hunt birds out there, once. But when the highway got built the birds left. Now nobody goes out there, it's just a piece of empty land the Interstate goes through."

"And I don't want to drive up at midnight and stand outside my car and get shot to pieces."

"No," Sapp said. "Here's where you want me to be."

With his pencil Sapp marked a blue road that wound more or less parallel to Route 20, a mile or so to the north.

"Piece of the old state road," Sapp said. "Was the main drag before the Interstate. I can park over here." He made a small circle. "And walk in behind them. About a mile maybe, mile and a half."

Sapp poured me some more coffee. I stirred in cream and sugar and I took another donut.

"When you have a couple donuts," Sapp said, "you know you've eaten something."

"Figured you for a dozen raw eggs a day," I said.

"And a good case of salmonella. I don't believe all that protein crap. You do the work, you get the muscle."

"Good," I said. "Gimme another one."

"I'll plan to get there early."

"Yes," I said. "Might be nice to walk the mile and a half in daylight."

"Yep. Country's not real rough, but there's trees and some ground cover. Easier in the light."

We drank coffee and cleaned up the last of the donuts. It was a little after eight-thirty in the morning.

"I got a vest," Sapp said. "Left over from my cop days."

"Thanks," I said. "I know this isn't your fight."

"I'm sure the bastards are homophobes," Sapp said.

"I'm sure they are," I said.

Sapp disappeared again and came back with a dark blue Kevlar vest.

"If Delroy's there," I said, "let's try not to kill him."

"Man," Sapp said, "you spoil everything."

"I know," I said. "But if he's alive I can turn him in and the thing is done."

"Business before pleasure," Sapp said. "What you should do is get something that's not obvious, and put it on the roadside at the twenty-mile spot, so I'll have a marker when I come in from the back."

I stood, and picked up the vest.

"I'll buy a cheap tire," I said, "and put it there. People see old tires on the highway all the time."

"I'll look for it," Sapp said. "You want a kiss good-bye?"

"From you?"

"Yes."

"I'd rather die," I said.

FIFTY-SIX

I WAS RESTLESS the rest of the day. I cleaned both my guns—the short-barreled .38 I usually carried, and the Browning nine-millimeter I had for high-volume backup. I reloaded both guns, and thumbed cartridges into an extra clip for the nine. I tried on the vest. Sapp and I were more or less the same size, so the vest fit. I did some push-ups. I stood in the motel doorway and looked up at the sky, which by midafternoon had begun to darken. I turned on the television set and found The Weather Channel. After about fifteen minutes of learning far more than I ever cared to know about a low-pressure area in the Texas panhandle, I heard them prophesying rain in Georgia. I did some more push-ups. I called Susan and, using a flawless southern accent, left a sexually explicit message on her answering machine. I took a walk. After the walk I went to the motel coffee shop and had a ham and cheese sandwich and a glass of milk. It started to rain. I stood in the doorway of my room and watched it for a while. It was a nice rain, steady but not too aggressive. Falling straight. The weather cooled. I took a nap.

When I woke up the afternoon had begun to turn into evening and the rain was unyielding. I took a shower and put on clean clothes and checked both guns again. The meeting on Route 20 could be a feint, of course, and they in fact intended to buzz me as I walked to my car to drive out there. Probably not. It was probably too clever for Delroy. But probably is not the same as certainly. If they intended to do that, how soon would they show up? Probably about ten-thirty. I thought about another sandwich, but I wasn't hungry. I had coffee instead. I didn't want to be sleepy later on. Then I went back to my room and strapped on both guns. The Browning I wore behind my right hipbone. The .38 I wore butt forward in front of my left hipbone. I put the extra clip in my hip pocket and a handful of .38 special ammunition in my pants pocket. Then, carrying the vest over my arm, I walked to my car and got in and pulled out of the parking lot. Nobody followed me. It was about nine o'clock—too early.

I drove out Route 20 to the designated spot. Maybe a mile before I got there there was a rest stop where a few cars and a lot of trailer trucks were parked. If I had been planning this, I'd have had a car with a car phone waiting, and as I approached I would have had the tail car that had followed me from the motel call, and when I went by, the second would pull out and follow me, and when I stopped, the two cars would park in front and behind at an angle, blocking me. They'd have to be a lot more alert now, since I had left too early, and they had apparently not counted on that. Maybe it would throw them and they'd call it off. I didn't want that. At the next exit I turned around and headed back to Lamarr. I couldn't risk confusing them so much that they didn't make their try at me. They'd been stupid enough to announce this one. The next time they might not. I called Susan on my car phone.

When she answered I said, "Spenser, Mobil Unit South."

"Oh good," she said. "Someone claiming to be one of your body parts left me a disgusting message in a fake southern accent on my answering machine this afternoon, while I was healing people."

"Which body part?" I said.

"You know perfectly well which body part," she said.

"Did you hate the message?" I said.

"No."

We talked the rest of the way back to the motel. Pearl was fine. I thought I might come home soon. The weather was lovely in Boston. It was raining here. I missed her. She missed me. We loved each other. I said goodbye as I pulled back into the motel parking lot. After I hung up I felt completed, the way I always did after talking to her, like a plant that had been watered.

It was ten-thirty. There was a car in the lot that hadn't been there when I'd left. A maroon Dodge, with a spotlight on the driver's side. This meant nothing. Cars come and go all the time in a motel parking lot. Still, there it was. I stayed in my car with the motor running, and the wipers going so I could see. I parked away from other cars with my nose pointing at the highway so that I couldn't be boxed in and shot in my car. I decided it was better than driving aimlessly up and down Route 20. I took out the nine, racked the slide back and pumped a round into the chamber, let the hammer down gently, and laid it in my lap. Nothing happened. At eleven I thought maybe driving aimlessly up and down Route 20 was better. At eleven-thirty, I slipped into the vest, tightened the straps, shrugged into a light wind-breaker, wheeled my car out of the parking lot in a leisurely manner, and drove toward the highway entrance with the nine still in my lap. As I went up the ramp, I saw the maroon Dodge come out of the lot and follow along in the same direction. The drive wasn't aimless anymore. We had begun.

The headlights made the wet highway shimmer. The moon was hidden. There were no streetlights. The weather was not a plus. A bright night would have been better. But it was a business in which you didn't always get to choose.

At seven minutes to midnight I pulled over onto the shoulder of the road near the designated spot. My tire, the marker for Tedy Sapp, was still where I'd thrown it, shiny in the rain. As I parked, a car passed me and pulled in at an angle in front of me. The maroon Dodge that had tailed me out pulled in behind. They were thinking right along with me. What little protection the car offered was outweighed by my immobility. I turned off the headlights and shut off the engine. I took the nine out of my lap and held it in my hand, close to my side. Then I got out, and closed the car door, and stood in the steady rain on the highway side of my car.

The headlights from the maroon Dodge brightened my part of the scene. The car ahead of me had shut off his lights. No one got out of either car. Except for the sound the rain made and the sound of the windshield wipers on the maroon Dodge, there was silence. Then there was some sound from the woods beyond the shoulder; then Jon Delroy and two other guys came out of the darkness and into enough of the headlight so I could see them. Delroy stayed where he was. The other two guys fanned out on either side of him. Both had shotguns. One wore a yellow rain jacket, the other was coatless, with an Atlanta Braves hat jammed down over his ears. There were no Security South uniforms visible.

"Spenser," Delroy said.

"Delroy."

As we spoke the driver of the Dodge got out to my right, and the driver of the car in front got out to my left. Observing peripherally, I was pleased that they didn't have shotguns.

"You wouldn't leave it alone," Delroy said.

"It's why I get the big bucks," I said.

"Was it you broke into the office in Atlanta?"

I smiled at him. I was trying for enigmatic, but it was raining hard and there were five guys with guns, so I may not have succeeded.

Delroy shrugged.

"Doesn't matter," he said. "Walk over here."

"So you can tell me who killed Walter Clive?"

"You know who killed Walter Clive," Delroy said. "Walk over here."

"Nope."

Delroy shrugged again. He seemed perfectly at ease. Every inch the commander.

"Die where you want to," Delroy said.

He pointed at the two men on my side of the car with the index finger of each hand and nodded once. Immediately there was a loud gunshot, but it came from the dark woods behind Delroy. The gunman to my right spun half around and his handgun clattered into the middle of the highway. I dropped to a squat against the side of my car and, leaning against it, shot the gunman to my left in the middle of the mass. He doubled up and fell on his side, crying in pain. I heard his gun skitter into the passing lane. I slid up the side of the car and brought my handgun down on top of the roof. The two men with shotguns were turning toward the gunshot when the gun fired from the woods again and one of them went down, staggered backwards against the Dodge by the force of the bullet. The other one, the guy in the Atlanta Braves hat, threw the shotgun away and started running west along the highway shoulder. Delroy seemed frozen. He hadn't even gotten his gun up. I went around the car and took it from his apparently paralyzed hand. He offered no resistance. Behind me the guy I'd shot kept crying in pain. I hated the sound. But there was nothing I could do about it, and it was better than me crying in pain. Tedy Sapp came out of the woods wearing a long black slicker and a black cowboy hat, and carrying an M1 rifle. I looked at the rifle.

"An oldie but goodie," I said.

"Like me," Sapp said.

FIFTY-SEVEN

BECKER AND I were in the interrogation room at the Columbia County Sheriff's substation chatting with Jon Delroy and Penny Clive.

Delroy sat with his hands folded on top of the shabby oak table that stood between him and Becker. Penny sat beside him, her legs crossed, her hands in her lap, her small white straw purse sitting on the edge of Becker's desk. I leaned on the green cinder-block wall to Becker's left, admiring Penny's demure exposure of tan thigh.

"Thanks for coming," Becker said to Penny.

"What's this all about, Dalton?" Penny said.

"That's what we're trying to find out. Mr. Spenser here says that Delroy attempted to kill him. Jon doesn't say anything. I know he's employed by you, so I thought maybe you could help us with this."

"You're not arresting me," Penny said.

It was said pleasantly, just clarifying.

"No, no. Just hoping you can help us get Mr. Delroy to explain his behavior."

Delroy looked at Penny and said softly, "We need a lawyer."

"Are you saying you'd like me to get you a lawyer, Jon?" Penny said. Her big eyes were wide and compassionate.

"We both need one," Delroy said, still softly, with a little emphasis on "both."

"I don't think I need one, Jon," Penny said.

Delroy nodded silently and didn't say anything else. Becker tipped back in his chair.

"Anybody like a Coca-Cola? Coffee? Glass of water?"

Nobody said anything. Becker nodded to himself.

"Now I hope you are not going to argue with me here, Jon," Becker said, "when I tell you that we got your ass. Excuse me, Penny."

Delroy didn't answer.

"Not only Mr. Spenser here but a reliable former police officer named Tedy Sapp witnessed your attempt to kill Mr. Spenser."

Penny frowned. *How terrible!*

"Tedy Sapp's a goddamned queer," Delroy said.

"Don't have much to do with his reliability as a witness," Becker said. "You are looking at a long time inside."

Becker shifted a little in his chair, getting more comfortable. Delroy didn't move or speak. His clasped hands were perfectly still, resting on the table.

"What I'd like to know is why you tried to kill Mr. Spenser?"

"You charging me?" Delroy said.

"Not yet," Becker said. "You used to be a police officer. You know when we charge you we got to read you your rights and let you get a lawyer, and the lawyer won't let you say anything, and we got no chance of working anything out together."

"So I could just get up and walk out of here?"

Becker didn't say anything for a moment. He looked at me. I got off the wall and walked over and leaned against the door. Becker smiled.

"Course you could," Becker said.

Delroy looked at me and back at Becker and didn't move.

"Dalton," Penny said, "I don't see what purpose I'm serving here."

"We was hoping you might urge Mr. Delroy to be forthright," Becker said.

"Well, of course. Jon, I do hope you'll be completely open with Sheriff Becker on this."

Delroy smiled a very small private smile and didn't say anything. He seemed intent on the knuckles of his folded hands.

"Maybe you could even tell us what he was supposed to be doing while he was off trying to kill Mr. Spenser," Becker said. "Sort of what was his official assignment?"

"Well, Jon didn't have any assignments, per se," Penny said. "He and his men provided security for our family and our business."

"The business being Three Fillies," Becker said.

Penny nodded yes.

"And the family being you and your two sisters."

"Yes."

"As I recall, Spenser had to rescue the two sisters from the security Mr. Delroy was providing," Becker said.

"Mr. Spenser was working under a misapprehension. My sisters were not, at the time he stole them from me, nor, I suspect, are they now, capable of caring for themselves, nor of making decisions in their best interest."

Becker nodded cheerily.

"We can get to that," Becker said. "You got any idea why Mr. Delroy attempted to murder Mr. Spenser?"

"None at all," Penny said.

"Jon," Becker said. "You interested in a shorter sentence?"

Delroy smiled again to himself, fleetingly. He looked at Penny. She didn't look at him. He returned his gaze to the backs of his folded hands.

"Okay," Becker said. "Mr. Spenser, would you open that door and ask Jerry to send those folks in?"

I stopped leaning on the door, and opened it, and stuck my head out, and nodded at the deputy and jerked a thumb toward the interrogation room, and closed the door again.

"You didn't by any chance ask Mr. Delroy to shoot Mr. Spenser, did you, Penny?"

"Dalton, that's offensive," Penny said. She was sitting straight upright in her chair. Her legs were not crossed anymore. Her knees were together, and her ankles. Her feet were flat on the floor.

"Yep," Becker said. "It is. Sorry about that, but it kind of looks to us as if you might have."

Penny pressed her lips together. The door opened behind me. I stepped to the side and, shepherded by a uni-
formed deputy, the Clive family circus trooped in
silently: Stonie, SueSue, Pud, Cord, Dolly Hartman, Jason Hartman, and, making a special guest appearance,
direct from San Francisco, Sherry Lark. Penny stared at
her mother, but didn't say anything. The deputy
arranged chairs and got everybody seated. He had a big
mustache like an old-time western lawman.

"Stand by, Jerry," Becker said to him, and the deputy
went and leaned on the wall I'd recently vacated when I
went to lean on the door.

"I want to thank you all for coming," Becker said.
"Especially you, Ms. Lark. I know it's a long flight."

"You sent me a ticket," she said.

Becker nodded.

"We had a little extra in the budget this month," he
said. "Now, so we're clear, no one is here under duress.
No one is under arrest, though it seems likely that Mr.
Delroy will be."

Penny was still looking at her mother. Delroy was
still looking at his knuckles. Everyone else tried not to
look at anybody, except Pud. Who glanced at me and
winked. Becker looked around.

"Everybody all right?" he said. "Anybody like a
Coca-Cola? Coffee? Glass of water?"

Nobody did.

"Okay," Becker said. "Mr. Spenser, you been the one
raising most of the hell in this case, why don't you hold
forth a little bit for us."

Everyone turned their head and looked at me. I felt

like I should open with a shuffle ball change. I decided against it.

"Most of you," I said, "will know some of what I'm going to say, but knowing all of it is the trick. This isn't a court of law. I'm telling you what I believe. But I can prove most of it."

The deputy with the mustache shifted a little as he leaned against the wall. I could hear the creak of his gun belt when he did so.

"About thirty years ago," I said, "Walter Clive had an affair with Dolly Hartman. The result of that union was Jason Hartman."

Stonie and SueSue both turned their gaze simultaneously on Jason. Everyone else kept looking at me.

"No one acknowledged that. Clive as far as I can tell didn't even know it. Dolly felt in the long run it would be in both her and Jason's best interests to lie back in the weeds and wait. Clive later made a will. It provided that his entire estate be equally divided among his children. Stonie and SueSue weren't too interested in the business. But Penny was, and she became more and more a part of it until she was really running things and Walter spent most of his time entertaining clients and traveling with Dolly, who resurfaced once Sherry was gone."

Everyone was still. Sherry Lark leaned forward a little, her mouth slightly open, frowning slightly to show how attentive she was being. There were probably very few unscripted moments in Sherry's life.

"I don't know what caused Dolly to bring it up when she did, and frankly, it doesn't matter much. But she eventually told Clive that Jason was his son. Clive was not a guy who had just fallen off the feed wagon as it trundled through town. He wanted proof. So they arranged with a doctor named Klein—most of you know him, I think—for a DNA test. Meanwhile Walter, in the eventuality that the test proved out, began talking to his lawyer, Rudy Vallone, about changing his will. The change would have included Jason in the estate, but, and here's the kicker, it would also have given him control of Three Fillies."

The silence in the room was cavernous. Delroy remained immobile, looking at his knuckles. I thought I could see the lines deepening around Penny's mouth as if she were clamping her jaw tighter. Jason Hartman was quiet and elegant, comfortable in the kind of serene way people have when they are getting their due.

"The DNA testing was a secret. The only people who knew were Dolly, and Walter and the doctor. Even Jason didn't know. He thought he was just getting a routine physical. However, as luck would have it, Dr. Klein and Sherry Lark had a, ah, relationship that transcended their casual medical acquaintance, and even better, so did Rudy Vallone and Sherry Lark. And, free spirit that she is, she used those relationships to find out that Walter was being tested to see if Jason was his son, and that Walter was thinking of changing his will in favor of Jason if the tests proved out."

I paused and looked at Sherry. On her face was perhaps the first genuine expression I'd ever seen there in our brief acquaintance. She looked scared.

"And she told Penny," I said.

Somebody, I think it was Dolly, inhaled audibly. No one else did anything.

Becker said, "You do that, Sherry?"

When Sherry answered, her voice was so constricted it was barely audible.

"Yes," she squeaked.

Slowly, as if it were choreographed, everyone in the room looked from Sherry to Penny.

FIFTY-EIGHT

- - - - - - - - - - - - - - - - - - - -

PENNY'S FACE WAS a little tight. Otherwise she seemed calm. Delroy glanced over at her.

"You need a lawyer," he said.

"You may need one, Jon. I do not."

"You killed Daddy," Stonie said. Her voice was very small.

"Stonie, try not to be an idiot," Penny said.

"You did," Stonie said in the small voice. "And you sent my husband away."

"Your husband?" Penny said. "Your pederast husband?"

Cord didn't look at anybody. Becker showed nothing, sitting back a little in his chair, listening.

"You destroyed my marriage and locked me up and tried to brainwash me," Stonie said. She was implacable in her small way, her voice somehow more absolute for being small.

"You did," SueSue said.

She was louder, as she always was. But it was sincere. Penny looked first at Stonie and then at SueSue. Her voice was flat when she spoke.

"You," Penny said to SueSue, "are married to a drunken philanderer, and have become a drunken philanderer too." She shifted her gaze onto Stonie. "And you are married to a homosexual child molester, and have yourself become a whore." She gazed at them with a look that seemed to encompass Cord and Pud too. It was a very cold gaze. Scary almost, unless of course, you were a tough guy like me. "My family," she said. "Whores, drunks, and perverts. You don't do anything. You don't contribute anything. You simply suck sustenance out of us like a cluster of parasites."

I looked at Becker. He was listening quietly. There was a hint of satisfaction in the set of his mouth.

"Penny," Delroy said.

"Shut up," she said. "You've caused a ridiculous amount of trouble."

Delroy nodded, as if in agreement with some inner voice. He went back to studying his hands. Penny returned her attention to her sisters.

"You should be thanking me," she said. "I couldn't do anything when Daddy was alive. His precious married daughters, let them do what they want to, as long as they're married. Leave them alone. Take care of them. If they get in trouble have Delroy erase it. Why do you think we kept Delroy around so long? To keep the sty clean."

"And then Daddy died," Becker said gently.

"And I tried to clean the sty for good. Get rid of the

husbands that were perverting them. Teach them, force them if necessary, to be clean."

"Like you," Becker said, even more softly.

I knew he was trying to channel the flow. It was a gamble. There was always the danger that it could interrupt the flow and she'd realize where she was going and stop. But Delroy hadn't been able to stop her, and I agreed with Becker. She couldn't stop, and maybe she could be directed.

"Yes," she said impatiently, "just like me. For God's sake, I was the perfect daughter. Pretty, smart, always helpful, good with the business, charming to everybody. Daddy used to say it was like I had a different set of genes." She smiled for a moment. It wasn't a pleasant thing to see. "And the sonovabitch didn't even prefer me. He liked those two useless cows as much as he liked me."

It all had a rehearsed quality, as if she were speaking from memory of a grievance that she had recited to herself a thousand times. And then she stopped, as if that were all she remembered. No one spoke. I heard the deputy's gun belt creak again as he shifted his weight a little. Becker looked at me.

"And then you found out he might give away the business," I said. "So you and Delroy invented the horse shootings. Just the kind of smart thing a gifted amateur might invent. And you had to smile and go along with it when your father hired me to look into things. You even chewed Delroy out in front of me, to make it look like you were with me all the way."

"And why on earth would Mr. Delroy go along with so harebrained a scheme?" Penny said.

She was quite rigid in her posture, and her mouth seemed stiff when she spoke. But her voice was perfectly calm.

"Because you and he were lovers," I said.

Penny laughed. It was, if possible, less pleasant than her smile had been.

"Mr. Delroy and I? Please. He was my employee, nothing more."

"And he was following your orders when he, ah, sequestered your sisters?"

"Yes."

"And when he tried to kill me?"

"No."

"Why did he try to kill me?" I said.

"I have no idea. Perhaps he killed my father and felt you were about to find that out."

"Actually, I was about to find out that *you* killed him."

"I did not," she said.

"And you think Delroy did?"

"I don't know. You asked me a question, I offered a supposition. I don't know why Mr. Delroy does what he does."

"You love him?" I said.

"Don't be ridiculous."

"You figure that means no, Sheriff?" I said.

Becker nodded slowly.

"I'd take it as that," he said. "You got a thought on all of this, Jon?"

Delroy didn't look up. He shook his head slowly.

"That's too bad," Becker said. "I was hoping maybe

you'd want to argue some of the points Ms. Clive made."

Delroy didn't respond. There was an odd half-smile fixed on his face.

"Well, think on it, Jon. 'Cause we are about to arrest you, and charge you with attempted murder, and put you away for a hell of a long time, unless you got something to bargain."

Delroy looked up then, his half-smile frozen in place, and turned his head slowly and stared at Penny Clive.

"I got nothing to bargain," he said.

Becker nodded slowly again.

"Too bad," he said. "Ms. Clive, I believe you killed your father or conspired with Delroy to do so. I was hoping he'd turn on you, but he don't seem ready to. So you can go."

Penny didn't say a word. She simply stood, and picked up her purse.

"'Course, just because he won't turn on you now," Becker said, "don't mean he won't do it later."

Penny walked to the door.

"And even if he don't," Becker said, "I will spend some time every day trying to catch you. I'm slow, sure enough, but in the long run I'm pretty good at this kind of work."

Penny looked back at him for a moment, and then opened the door and went out without shutting it.

"Jerry," Becker said. "You can take all these folks out except Mr. Delroy."

Everyone stood up. No one had anything to say, not even Pud, who was normally as repressible as a goat.

When we were alone, Becker said, "Jon Delroy, you are under arrest for attempted murder. You have the right to remain silent . . ."

"I know," Delroy said. "Don't bother."

Becker plowed right on through the whole Miranda recitation without pause. When he was through listening to the recitation of his rights, Delroy sat perfectly still for a moment. Then without looking at either me or Becker, he spoke to us both.

"I been scamming women all my life," he said. "This one time, I fell in love."

"Bad timing," I said.

Delroy shrugged.

ROBERT B. PARKER

Gunman's Rhapsody

A NOVEL

PUTNAM

Robert B. Parker

Perish Twice

PUTNAM